The Anatomy of Flying Things

The Anatomy of Flying Things

Short Stories

Published by Afritondo Media and Publishing 2023

First published in Great Britain in 2023
by Afritondo Media and Publishing
Preston, United Kingdom
www.afritondo.com

ISBN: 978-1-7394902-0-1

For all those who seek to discover the world

CONTENTS

It is a child who has never traveled who says that only his mother prepares tasty meals.

African proverb

THE MAN FROM ABẸ̀ÒKUTA
Ayo Awoyungbo

He was meandering down Holloway Road when the 43 sneaked by, brake lights blinking as it slowed for the next stop. About sixty yards behind and with a lone passenger waiting, the odds were not in his favour, so he muttered, 'Get the next one', and continued his leisurely stroll. Then, for reasons he couldn't quite explain, he changed his mind and broke into a sprint, arriving just after the doors closed. In case anyone was watching, he half-turned and jogged on the spot, pretending he didn't want it anyway. Seated downstairs near the back, a smartly dressed couple caught his eye and smiled knowingly. For safety reasons, bus drivers are instructed not to reopen the doors after servicing a stop. That the bus company risks a fine does nothing to dilute the acute mixture of disappointment and embarrassment felt by the just-missed-it commuter recovering from a frantic dash. But sometimes, if the bus hasn't fully departed because it's waiting for a gap in traffic, the driver may show mercy. It was August, humid, and with his white button-down shirt already damp at the armpits, Gbenga was grateful when the doors sprang open. Even if there's no place you have to be, it's nice to have the effort rewarded. He jumped on, slightly out of breath, mouthing 'thanks' and 'sorry' as he fumbled in his pockets for his Oyster card and tapped it on the reader.

'Kòsí wàhálà, oṣé' said the driver, a middle-aged white man, easing the bus smoothly into the steady stream of slow-moving vehicles.

Gbenga made his way upstairs and headed for the rear. There were three other people—two teenage girls in the middle and a man at the front engrossed in a newspaper. Flinging himself into the corner of the last row, he planted his satchel on the next seat to stake his claim. If vacant, this was where he always sat, Owner's Corner.

Unbidden, thoughts of Sarah filled his mind. He remembered their first time on the bus together. They had not been dating long, and he felt obliged to explain.

'Unless driving, a car owner must sit diagonal to the chauffeur in the corner directly behind the front passenger seat. It makes no difference whether the vehicle is tear rubber or Tokunbo—'

'Tear rubber? Tokunbo?' She interrupted his flow.

'Tear rubber means brand new, and Tokunbo is imported second-hand,' he clarified impatiently. 'Owner's Corner is more than just some trivial perk for buying a car. It's an inalienable right.'

She was fascinated. 'But we're on the bus?'

He'd smiled, imagining himself in the back of a G-Wagon. 'No condition is permanent for a future big man.'

'Or woman.'

He'd nodded. 'When the cops pull you over, the initial clash with the driver is foreplay, but it's the owner who provides satisfaction.'

'You mean, like, give them money?'

That she had laughed when he said, 'You'll be a Nigerian soon,' was a good sign.

I'm not thinking about Sarah today, Gbenga decided, returning to the present. He made himself comfortable. 'Air conditioning, great,' he observed to no one in particular, then, 'not too bad, not too bad' as the man-made breeze cooled him.

He'd been talking to himself for long enough now for it to be considered a habit. He was self-conscious rather than ashamed and believed that a problem shared, even with oneself, was a problem halved. He usually kept his voice low, aware that people who looked like him were overrepresented in psychiatric wards and that speaking aloud with no visible audience was guaranteed to attract unwanted attention. Thankfully, to most casual observers, he was probably making or receiving a call using a Bluetooth earpiece. This assumption provided excellent cover because as the frequency of his solo conversations increased, so did the chances of misunderstandings. The most recent was in the supermarket. He'd been at the self-checkout, scanning his groceries and grumbling about rising prices, when a supervisor approached. She was young, with shoulder-length blonde hair and a friendly, open face.

'Uncle, ṣé ẹ wà okay?' she enquired.

Beep by beep, Gbenga placed six tins of own-brand rice pudding in the bagging area. He realised she must have been watching him, and it triggered humiliating memories of being spied on and followed by suspicious store security staff. Shopping while black was still, occasionally, a blood sport, but being profiled in a supermarket was a new low.

She tried again. 'You alright? You know you can just scan one and do "times 6"?'

He brandished a tin and raised his voice. 'Last week, this was 23 pence. I don't need your help when I'm not stealing.'

A few shoppers paused, anticipating drama. When there was none, they continued shopping. From his station at the store entrance, the bored security guard glanced over and, still bored, returned to his screen.

The self-service supervisor rolled her eyes. 'Sir, there's no need to shout. I thought you were talking to me, and I was only doing my job.' She kissed her teeth, muttering, 'Abájọ! Wọ́n ṣó pe wèrè aláṣọ ló pòjù London. When they look normal, how can we tell they're not?' as she retreated.

He ignored her, tapping his bank card on the screen when requested by the machine. 'I wasn't,' he thought. 'I was talking to me.'

That was perhaps a fortnight ago; it was becoming difficult to keep track of time. Gbenga's self-directed conversation provided an outlet for intrusive thoughts. It also relieved his stress, so even when his monologue was out loud, as long as nobody noticed, he wasn't worried. Of much greater concern were the random white people speaking to him in Yoruba. Like that blonde supervisor who'd insulted him in the supermarket. And the bus driver.

I own this bus. I travel on it every day. Smoking on buses is prohibited and punishable by a fine or cancer. But they'll have to catch me first.

Rush hour was over. Gbenga lit the spliff he'd rolled earlier: spliff number one—because this was a two-spliff journey. He slouched low in his seat, pressing his shoulders into the hard cushion and jamming his knees against the back of the empty row in front to make himself less visible. He had taken his medication that morning and brought it along. Without lowering his knees, he squeezed his hand into the front pocket of his jeans, murmuring, 'Just for reassurance, just for reassurance,' as he caressed the small box of pills squashed in with keys, coins, and a super-thin silver Rizla.

The teenage girls twisted around when they heard his voice, whispering and sniggering. He stopped rummaging in his pocket and scowled, lowering his legs with a thud. 'Can I help you?' he barked. They immediately looked away. The blonde pressed the bell for the next stop and studied her phone intently.

Gbenga took a long drag, held it, then exhaled. The man at the front turned sharply as the skunky odour of marijuana filled the air. He made a big thing of opening a window, exaggeratedly fanning with his newspaper. Their eyes met. Gbenga: hostile; aggressive. The man's eyes were narrowed and inquisitive. Each held the other's gaze, unblinking, as they segued into an impromptu staring contest.

Say something. Or come on if you're hard enough.

The bus came to a halt. Someone whistled the opening bars to the theme from 'The Good, the Bad, and the Ugly.' It may have been the blonde girl. The other girl giggled and tried to shush the blond girl as they clattered down the stairs. The man returned to his newspaper, leaving Gbenga disappointed. He would have relished any human contact, even violence.

The morning had settled into that post-rush hour, pre-prandial lull when time itself seems to pause for breath. It was quiet, save for the rhythm of tyres on tarmac and the low hum of the acoustic vehicle alerting system—that artificial noise made by electric buses travelling at a low speed. Pulling idly on his spliff, Gbenga marvelled as the acrid smoke escaped his nostrils and hung in the air in Rorschach patterns. The warm sunlight, reflected through the windows, induced a pleasant torpor, and he rested his head against the glass. In the hush, the number 43 tiptoed along City Road, dodging roadworks and sidestepping pedestrians.

The man at the front shattered the peace. 'May I talk to you for a moment?'

His measured tone betrayed no accent. Without waiting for a reply, he got up and walked towards the back, a leather satchel swinging from one shoulder. Gbenga watched him approach. He was about 5-foot, 10 inches tall, slim, and neatly dressed in a long-sleeved white shirt with a button-down collar and black jeans. Once near, he unceremoniously picked up Gbenga's bag and placed it on a seat further along before plonking himself down beside him. Controlling his rage at the sheer audacity, Gbenga studied the man's face, the grizzled hair, the beard begging for a trim. Up close, he was older, with lines wrinkling the skin around his greyish-green eyes. 'Old enough to know better,' thought Gbenga indignantly. On public transport, the right to individual space and the strict observance of personal boundaries are sacrosanct. Of sins most cardinal, the uninvited touching of property belonging to another is second only to sitting next to a person you don't know when there are numerous empty seats. To avert a catastrophe of epic proportions, bus etiquette in London must be strictly observed. Everyone knows that.

Abi na pastor? Is he going to preach to me? Give a tract and piss off.

'Mate, you're in my personal space. What do you want? You need to get out of my face. And why did you move my bag?' Sitting upright, Gbenga blew weed fumes at him, keen to conclude this irritating encounter with the minimum of fuss.

Engulfed by second-hand smoke, the man did not blink. 'I'm definitely not an evangelist, peripatetic or otherwise. Now, what should we talk about?'

'Fuck knows. Move yourself! You got on my bus and are trying to provoke me into beating the shite out of you.' The spliff was dying, so Gbenga flicked the stub away, tensing as it bounced off the man's shirt and fell. He felt a rush of adrenaline.

How does he know I'm not carrying? Gut him like a fish, and they'll say crime in London. I bet the CCTV's not working—

'It's working. And you've never gutted a fish in your life,' replied the man. Unperturbed by the smear of ash on his hitherto pristine shirt, he winked.

'What the—?' spluttered Gbenga. *Wetin dey worry dis fool? Is he trying to cottage me?*

'I think you'll find the word is "cruise". But don't flatter yourself; you're not my type. You haven't got a knife, and you wouldn't stab me even if you did because (a) you're not a killer and (b) you're curious about who I am and what, if anything, I want from you.'

He had raised his left hand and used the right to count the thumb and index finger for (a) and (b). He wasn't smiling, but there was amusement in his tone.

'What do you want? Have you got a death wish, or do you want to be a statistic?' yelled Gbenga, wiping his sweaty hands on the front of his black jeans. He was starting to freak out at the way the man seemed to be incorporating his thoughts into the conversation. *How is he answering what I'm thinking? Am I saying things out loud?* He was also peeved that his voice came out a tad higher than intended.

The man simply smirked.

'I don't have to deal with this shit,' Gbenga spat, his bravado rapidly draining. He stood, but restricted by the narrow space between rows, bumped against the man's leg in an attempt to barge past and sit elsewhere. *Why fight when you can walk away?*

'Darling, I barely know you,' quipped the man as their knees touched. 'Okay, look, I'm just messing with you. I know you're obsessed with blonde girls. I'm just messing with you, really.' He raised his smooth pale hands to chest level, palms out in a placatory gesture. 'Why don't you sit down and quit the gangster act? Just because your friends call you "G" doesn't mean you are.'

He noted Gbenga's dazed hesitation and added 'please' with a polite smile. He put his satchel on the seat where he had placed Gbenga's: it was obvious he expected compliance.

'Do I know you? How do you know my friends call me G?' Reluctantly, Gbenga sat. He was wary, wondering whether this was the beginning of some new scam, one he hadn't heard of. He also felt queasy and was worried that he might throw up. To maintain some sort of equilibrium, he stared at the small burn above the man's right cuff, courtesy of a stray ember from the discarded spliff.

'Just breathe, G, you'll be fine,' said the man. 'There's no cause for alarm. I'm not trying to swindle you out of your life savings.' He bent his head and lowered his voice, ready to share a secret. 'But it might be a good idea to change your password from G4321mEd!c. That's capital G for golf, four, three, two, one, lower case m, upper case E, lower case d, exclamation mark, lower case c.' He slowly shook his head. 'With a weak password like that for telephone banking, you're just asking for it.' Gbenga's chest tightened as the man continued. 'And no worries about the shirt, son—I've plenty. What's more important is why you have decided to waste your life.'

Gbenga exploded. 'What? Who the hell are you to tell me about my life? What do you know about me? And don't ever call me son.' Furious, confused, and stuttering all at once, he resisted an illogical urge to whip out his wallet and check his bank card. *How can this guy read my thoughts? How does he know my password? This is not happening.*

He was starting to lose it, so he grabbed the front of the man's shirt and yanked him forward, snarling, 'Who are you? How do you know my password?'

The man did not push back or attempt to break Gbenga's hold. Keeping both arms loose at his sides, he let himself be dragged closer until their faces were inches apart. Gbenga raised his fist.

'Your call,' said the man, unflinching.

He couldn't do it. The lack of resistance and his unreadable face made punching him impossible. Deflated, he let his right arm drop. Gbenga's left hand was still holding onto his collar, so the man calmly pushed it away. He smoothed his wrinkled shirt carefully. If he was frightened, it wasn't obvious. Gbenga suddenly realised something odd about the man's hands: there were no palmar creases on either, and his fingers had no horizontal lines at the proximal, middle, and distal phalanges. No lines on the thumbs. Nothing. The hands protruding from his shirt sleeves looked unreal, like badly made prostheses or flesh-coloured gloves fashioned from unblemished skin.

'Gbenga, Gbenga, Gbenga,' chided the man, shaking his head, voice and gesture conveying sorrow and exasperation in equal measure. Delicately wiping a fleck of Gbenga's spittle from his cheek, he produced an unopened plastic bottle of water from his bag.

'Go on, it's only water, and it's time for your medication.' He put the bottle on the seat between them.

Gbenga couldn't remember removing his pills from his pocket. The man gently pried the box from his unsteady grip, opened it, and broke off a row from the small plastic sheet. He placed the box next to the water.

'There you go.'

Gbenga popped the blister pack, and two pills fell into his hand. He swallowed them together and grabbed the water, swigging it and spilling some down his shirt.

'You're welcome,' said the man, waving away the bottle.

Like trapped birds colliding with a plate-glass window, thoughts crashed against Gbenga's skull. *Na me be dis? He knows my name and password and that I'm on medication. He has weird hands and can read my mind. I should stop thinking so he won't know what I'm thinking. Why hasn't anyone come upstairs since I entered this bus? At least he hasn't asked how many times he called me—*

'Better? Now, how many times did I call you?'

'Three times.' Gbenga nodded weakly. 'Who *are* you?'

'Who are *you*? Gbenga Adelayo, a third-year escapee from the University of Edinburgh Medical School. You absconded two months ago, ostensibly as a result of a quarrel with your girlfriend Sarah, but you had been thinking about abandoning your course anyway because you can't take the pressure.'

All undergraduate medical students do a Bachelor of Medical Sciences (BMedSci) in the third year of the MBChB programme. The purpose of this intercalated year is to provide an opportunity to study an area of interest, learn new skills and experience aspects of academic medicine. But it's tough, and my research into universal health coverage is not going well. I should have stuck with neural networks and prosthetics.

The man was self-assured and matter-of-fact. 'She's worried sick because you won't pick up her calls and have not been in contact since you left. Sarah's reported you missing to the university authorities and Edinburgh Police, accusing the latter of racism because she doesn't think they're doing enough to find you. Your parents in Nigeria believe you are still in Edinburgh, unaware that you are on medication and have taken this unapproved leave of absence. You've depleted your savings renting a room in a shared house in Archway, feeding yourself when you can be bothered, and buying weekly Oyster cards so that you can spend your days aimlessly riding this bus, which, for some reason, you think you own.'

It was not clear whether he had paused or finished. But there was silence.

'How do you know all this?'

'It's true, isn't it?'

Resigned to his imminent death, Gbenga fired up his other spliff on the third attempt, the plastic lighter trembling in his hand. Swallowing a lungful of smoke, he savoured it like a last request. He knew better than to offer it to the man. They both stared straight ahead, one with hands resting lightly on his knees, the other puffing like his life depended on it.

This is not a man. He's obviously a spirit sent to torment me. But he can't harm me. They say things sent from the village lose their potency once they cross the ocean. You know the Nollywood tropes: earthenware pots decorated with camwood, blood-splattered offerings wrapped in banana leaves bound with twine. And don't forget the Babaláwo somewhere in a forest, intoning ancient incantations. Why can't we have metaphors for a new generation? Surely, the Òrìṣàs must have modernised? Online access via an app and Bitcoin payments alongside palm oil and orógbó? And let's not even think about the possibilities of P2P networks—

'I've watched those films,' remarked the man conversationally. 'But representation is changing. You did your A-levels here, so you've been away for a minute. Art imitates life, and Nollywood 4.0 hits differently to keep pace with the culture.' He paused, a faraway look on his face. 'Me, I still love the classics: "Living in Bondage", "Nneka, the Pretty Serpent", and "Sakobi: The Snake Girl". All good films. I'm thinking originals, not remakes. But I digress.' He raised a peremptory hand, sensing Gbenga was about to interrupt. 'Old school things are old school things. And if they aren't broken, well, you know what they say. Oh, and as for blockchain, I couldn't possibly comment on its application to the binary code of Odù Ifá. Well above my pay grade.' Again, Gbenga tried to speak, but the man cut him off. 'G, you know what? Sometimes, things are old school for a reason, hmm?'

I'm at Àṣà jẹun in Peckham for my àbùlà fix. I've just introduced my gbẹ̀giri to the ewédú when boys on the next table drop one gist about some guy studying medicine in Edinburgh. Seven years later and now a Resident at Western General, he's acquired an Edinburgh accent, along with a blonde-haired girlfriend. He has no intention of returning home. Phone calls are ignored. Complete silence. All the parents want is to remind him of their financial sacrifice. Don't ask me the details; how would I know? Their son, the doctor, has hardened his heart and decided to live his life in Edinburgh. Can you blame him? All our doctors are leaving anyway—why would he go back? But something happens—let's just call it reverse jápá. According to the story, one night he bolts awake at the stroke of midnight and hears his name three times: Olúwagbémiga, Olúwagbémiga, Olúwagbémiga. I don't know whether the call wakes him or whether he's already awake and then hears the call. I don't know whether he answers. Abeg, your question

*too plenty, sef. You know, when they call you, it's not about the answer.
Old school things, right? The very next morning, he hands in his notice,
books a flight, and starts packing. Within three months he's back home;
the only evidence he was ever there the 'For Sale' sign outside his flat and
a heartbroken blonde Scottish doctor. He's married now and has a clinic
above a chemist in Abẹ̀òkuta.*

'True story,' averred the man. 'True true.'

Gbenga sat in stunned silence, trying to take it all in. The man
yawned. Lacing his fingers behind his neck, he massaged it to relieve
the cricks. Then he stretched out his legs and crossed his ankles. He
seemed to be smiling, although the corners of his mouth pointed
down. His face was mobile, with fleeting expressions—like ripples
on a lake—constantly altering his features.

'Son, you should go back. Think about the sacrifices your parents
are making. The very least you can do is answer their phone calls.
Think how proud they will be when you come home as a doctor
and open your own clinic in Abẹ̀òkuta. I hear Oke Mosan's good.'

His smile broadened when he said 'Abẹ̀òkuta', like he'd lived a
previous life in the shadow of the rock. 'That's where you're from,
abi?'

'You can read my mind. You know where I'm from. You even
have my bank account information.' Still in shock, Gbenga was
sullen. Then he had a flash of clarity. 'I'm dead, and you're Jesus,
right?'

The man let out a discordant laugh. There was something
disquieting about his small, evenly-spaced teeth.

'You think Jesus is white? Laugh out loud. Sorry, do people still
say that?'

'Fuck knows. Okay, am I asleep? Is this a dream?'

'Órẹ́, jí má sùn! Wake up, don't sleep! Maybe you should pinch
yourself? Don't pinch *me*; we've already done the physical violence

thing. And try to express yourself without swearing. Although you're getting an Edinburgh accent, you haven't lived there long enough to have gone completely native.'

Gbenga changed tack. 'What's your name? Who sent you? And why should I go back?'

The questions were ignored.

'G, you need to quit smoking. Really. Enough with the herb already. And stop feeling sorry for yourself. Get your shit together and finish your fucking education.'

'I thought you said—'

'Swearing is a powerful tool, but it's more effective when used sparingly.' The man sighed. 'Okay, listen, you're right. Why go back to a country where you'll be poorly paid, work in crap conditions, and make a fucking difference? Where later, you will establish your own hospital and work with others who share your vision of affordable healthcare for ordinary people?'

It suddenly dawned on Gbenga that the man was talking about returning to Nigeria, not just to Edinburgh. 'So, it's a hospital now? What happened to the clinic? And what about Sarah?'

'What about her? I thought you weren't sure she was 'the one'? Newsflash: she's not sure you are, either. And going AWOL won't have reassured her, will it?' He snorted. 'It's a clinic first; the hospital comes later. Use your common sense.'

'Wow! Insults too?'

'You're welcome. Look, it's not that deep. You don't have to do what everybody else does—just what *you* must do. And for now, all you have to do is plan a strategy rather than make hasty life decisions. What's the plan if you quit university—smoke weed and pop pills all day? Or ride this bus until you feel better?'

So much for my telepathic spirit guide or whatever you are. Don't give up the day job. I'm more depressed than ever.

'You just think you are. Don't wallow—it's unbecoming in a man your age. Make the changes required. Go back to Teviot Place and finish what you've started; choose life, like in the film.'

'What film?' asked Gbenga, intrigued.

'What do you mean, "what film?" Renton? Begbie? Oh, forget it. You can change your future with the things you do now. It's not written in stone or in the stars. You can change your fate. Or maybe it wasn't your destiny in the first place?'

With the last, the man put both hands in front of his face and wiggled his fingers, humming tunelessly while shaking his head from side to side. The backs of his hands were like his palms—completely smooth without knuckles or fingernails. Bluish veins glistened beneath the translucent flesh.

Gbenga slid down in his seat. *Why is he wiggling his fingers and humming? Is he going to disappear? What does it all mean?*

The man's eyes lit up, and he spoke excitedly, each word bumping into the next. 'Have you ever watched "The Twilight Zone"? No? Believe me, they're classics. Clearly before your time. "X Files" then? Mulder and Scully? You've never heard of them? You're in for a treat. Ah, I know, I know—"Black Mirror"? No, I'm not being racist. Bad joke, sorry. You don't have Netflix? Not to worry. Anyhow, "Black Mirror" is more of your near-future sci-fi tech dystopia as a vehicle for social commentary type series than out-and-out mystery.' He paused, looking sheepish. 'Apologies, I got somewhat carried away. Listen, just ignore me; you haven't a clue what I'm on about. All that matters is that I know you'll be a fantastic doctor.'

'How do you know?'

He arched an eyebrow. 'Not that you'd realise, but I just hummed the theme tune from "The Twilight Zone"—what more do you want? G, promise me you'll find time to educate yourself. There are loads of episodes on YouTube, not necessarily the best ones, but okay to start.' He became animated again, his pale hand balling into a fist and his voice rising. 'Come on, you enjoy SFF, FFS! See what

I did there? At least think about it.'

Gbenga tried again. 'So, you won't tell me who you are, what you are, or where you're from, and I'm supposed to just believe you?'

'I could tell you, but I'd have to kill me,' declared the man, deadpan. He was calm, and his mouth twitched almost imperceptibly, like he was stifling a laugh. 'You know, I've always wanted to say that, so thank you for the opportunity.' Bowing his head, he smiled his upside-down smile. 'Look, I'm just messing around. You have absolutely nothing to fear from me.' He raised his hands once more, and Gbenga watched the veins shimmer and swell, now the colour of molten lava. By some trick of the light, his fingers appeared acuminate, each stiletto-like digit suffused with a silvery red glow. They looked like they might be extremely hot.

'Your hands?' queried Gbenga.

'But that would defeat the whole purpose,' declared the man solemnly, lowering them and ignoring the question. 'Ọgbẹ̀rì, this is the day job. Supernatural, extra-terrestrial, or simply a figment of the imagination—whatever works best. It's entirely up to you.' Then he brightened. 'You know, on reflection, I may have hummed the theme tune from "The Outer Limits" rather than "The Twilight Zone"—an easy mistake as they're similar. The shows, not the theme tunes. But I made universally recognised finger movements to indicate things that surpass human understanding. I'll admit that the head movements were a bad idea, although given that we've been talking for over an hour and you still ask *how*, I can't pretend not to feel a little insulted.'

He did, in fact, sound hurt. 'Never mind,' he said. 'End of the road.'

The engine and upstairs lights switched off simultaneously, indicating their arrival at London Bridge Station, the last stop. Gbenga stood and brushed ash off his shirt, noticing for the first time the small burn just above the cuff on his right sleeve. Remaining seated, the man passed Gbenga his satchel; it was exactly the same as his. 'I hope he hasn't mixed them up,' Gbenga thought.

'I haven't. And don't thank me. Thank *you*. When you get back to Edinburgh, devise a study routine with plenty of downtime. Pace yourself. A pẹ́ kí ó tó jẹun, kìí jẹ ìbàjẹ: the person who eats late won't eat rotten food. Understand the proverb and don't rush things. And don't forget that you'll have to do something great—and by great, I mean expensive—to make amends with Sarah. It's a big ask, so give her plenty of time to get used to the idea of—'

'Living in Abẹ́òkuta,' Gbenga interjected, allowing himself a smile, his first since the journey began.

'Above the chemist,' the man finished, smiling too. 'I knew we'd get there in the end.'

'Yes, we will,' thought Gbenga, walking down the stairs and off the empty bus without a backward glance.

I'M TAKING IT TO THE GRAVE
C.M. Okonkwo

*Inspired by an online photo of Nigerian poet Mabel Segun in
Strasbourg, France, in 1983.*

Still eyes behind large-framed glasses on a prepossessing and petite lady stared back from the monochrome picture at the old woman holding it. The lady in the photograph was in the company of a white man, also in large-framed glasses, both sitting half a bum on a bollard in front of a building with glass doors. Her afro was full and all over the place like a wild shrub and shone black as if oiled with shoe polish. The sun, though grey, glared through the reflection on one of the glass doors as if it were its last day on Earth, yet the lady donned a leather jacket over an African-print dress. Her companion wore a sweater, a muffler hanging loosely around his neck.

Not a smile on either face, frigidity seeped out of the picture. It was impossible to tell if both were there by chance, choice, or something else. They gave nothing extra, just like the black and white tones of the picture. It must have been 1963 or thereabout, almost 60 years now, but nothing in the picture spoke of decades past, only the afro and the lack of colour. For all the old woman holding the picture could remember, it could have been any year. The memory of that day was blurry like the face of the person who had taken the shot. Her shrivelled fingers, shaky with each touch, lined the edges of the Polaroid. Back in her time, everyone wanted to own the camera— born seven years after her, in 1937, but became instant ten years later, printing within seconds of taking a shot. The old woman had not owned one, but whoever had taken the photo must have given it to her to treasure memories that had now been lost to the enemy called old age, leaving a void in its wake.

With the speed of a snail and the strength of a newborn, she flipped the photo over. No information, just black polaroid paper that had lost most of its gloss. The last proof of a long life, moving year to year, country to country, city to city, all photos misplaced but this one, preserved within the pages of a journal of poems she had both experienced and imagined and stories she did not want to forget.

She flipped through every page of the journal and found nothing about the picture. She had not thought back then that she might live this long or long enough to forget the story behind the photograph; otherwise, she would have written a story about it. Now it stared blankly at her without answers like a static television screen. She awoke abruptly from her potholed memory lane at the sound of a mild harrumph. It was not from her, but it had been done to get her attention. She looked up at a pair of young and eager eyes plastered on the curious face of an aspiring writer who reminded her of herself when the fire first burned within. The young girl, with a voice recorder in hand, was waiting for answers to how Stella Makun, an old woman from a small Yoruba village in Nigeria, came to write the best poems in the world, poems that married sweet and bitter, love and loss, elicited pleasant emotions and tears at the same time.

Everyone yearned to know whence the secret stream flowed, at least before the old woman shut her eyes one last time to the world and, with them, took along the untold story of her oeuvres. She wanted to take it to the grave, she had said when asked many years before, and that was fast becoming a reality for her at ninety. Many had come to her for the story but were disappointed, first by her not wanting to reveal it, then by her gradually forgetting it, and now by her struggling to recall it. Even if she took her head apart and looked inside, she would not remember what had driven her to abandon the sacrifices of her demanding parents to see their daughter become a renowned scientist, not a poet—one who would come to be celebrated and decorated and receive a Nigerian National Order of Merit Award, but a poet all the same. A more intentional clearing of the throat snapped the old woman back to the present. Her weary eyes travelled around her congested study, with more books than furniture, and settled on the giant ticking clock above the door. She prayed and hoped that she would be able to remember, one last time, if not for the young girl sat like a sculpture in front of her, refusing to blink and miss a moment, but for herself.

She shut her eyes and ran her fingers through the picture; still nothing came to her. She sighed in despair. When she opened her eyes, a spine-tingling cold hugged her. She looked around and was gripped by fear; in place of the young aspiring writer was a busy train station, and she was in the centre of it.

Her right hand felt heavy all of a sudden. A brown one-strap wooden box suitcase, shaped like a treasure chest, weighed it down. In her other hand was an off-white slip. She raised it to her face; it was a French train ticket from *Gare de L'Est* in Paris to *Gare de Strasbourg-Ville* in Strasbourg, and the date was *vendredi 20 décembre*, 1963. Confusion reared its head, though everything was beginning to look familiar. She knew where she was but not why or how she got there. An Orient Express train hooted on the tracks, warning of its imminent departure. Travellers scurried towards it from all directions, like pigeons scavenging for crumbs. Some jostled to climb in, holding on to their hats and other loose belongings; others, still on board, eager to descend, expertly squeezed their way out, carrying different shades and sizes of suitcases and holding the same off-white slip.

She looked at the slip again. She had made the trip to Paris the night before, a pre-Christmas gift from her parents for completing a master's degree and a ploy to get her to attend a gateway science conference for intending doctoral degree applicants. It was to be her first trip out of Nigeria, the one that would shape her in many unexpected ways. She looked at the slip again, unable to tell then that *vendredi* was Friday in French, and still could not tell now. It was at that moment she noticed it. Her hand. It looked young, like it was yet to feel life. She released her grip from the suitcase strap and looked at both her hands, side by side; she felt her body, neck, and face. Every bit of her felt young, her sagging skin held tightly as if stitched with fine thread.

The train hooted again, this time, the sound of departure, continuing its journey to another city. Her focus returned to the multitude in the station as they filed in and out. They walked beside and around her, each time avoiding her, not before casting her a side glance. She could not tell if they were shocked to see a woman in a print summer dress in the cold or if it was due to her puzzling resemblance to the sensational Josephine Baker, who did not wear an afro. She immediately felt her head. Her afro was still full and wild, just as it had been in the picture, just as it had been on that same day in 1963. Shivering, she picked up her suitcase and left the station. The cold was more intense at the other side of the door as if the city was buried within a chest freezer. The sun hid behind a stagnant cloud, though its full presence would not have made a difference.

The streets of Strasbourg looked like an art painting. Heavy bronze letters on a short ornate brick wall across the train station read *Bienvenue á Strasbourg*. It had mesmerised her then and still had the same effect now, even after touring the world for many years and seeing everything there was to see. The city was beautiful and bustling, with old-school vehicles littered about the streets, driven by men in tweed suits and gentleman's hats, and ladies with elaborate fur hats and boas taking passenger seats. Lamp posts had fairy string lights that stretched from one end of the street to the other, dropping down in layers like a chandelier. Street corners were decorated with flowers, reindeer, elves, carriages, and gift boxes, all carved from fairy lights. Fake pines were rooted on walkways, coiled with lines of miniature golden bells that jingled each time a mild wind swept through. The place smelled like holiday and celebration. Christmas was in the air.

She took in the scent, turned abruptly and moved to the side when a violent wind tore through the calm. She did not see the rapidly approaching figure who had burst out of nowhere with his head lowered, turning to the side to also avoid the wind. They collided. A paper cup of coffee flew off his hand and landed on the floor. Its contents emptied in seconds. A brown paper bag dropped to the ground, revealing freshly baked pastries. Her tummy growled at the sight. The man picked up what he could salvage, then narrowed his light-blue eyes at her as he towered over her. Perhaps he had expected an apology, but she did not give one. No one spoke.

'*Putain!*' he muttered through gritted teeth. It was a language she did not understand, but she could guess from his tone that he had cursed. He picked up the cup, tossed it in a rusty metal street litter can, and stormed off in the direction he had come. When she recovered from the shock and the soul-piercing light-blue eyes that had sent an unexpected chill through her, she mouthed 'I'm sorry' to the air. The chill reminded her that she was still outside and had to get to someplace warm. A quick search of her suitcase—which contained more impractical African-print dresses, underwear, and toiletries—and she found information on the hotel she was to stay in, tucked between her three-day return trip ticket to Lagos. Everything had already been planned. Now, she just had to get to the hotel. At the right-hand corner of the historicist-styled train station, she spotted a fleet of black Citroën DS 19 sedans with bold taxi signs atop, lined in front of several bistros bubbling with guests. Children sold lilies by the windows. Mendicants and homeless people solicited change from pedestrians who avoided eye contact with them and hurried off. Tricksters animated the minds of the curious. The city was on the move.

The sudden and elongated honk of a vehicle that almost ran over a dog took her mind back to the road. The dog owner apologised to the motorist and scolded the animal. She turned to the taxi line with much enthusiasm. She did not remember entering one back then, but she knew she could not have been this excited about entering an ordinary vehicle, but reliving the experience now felt like a mind-blowing adventure. She approached the road and looked both ways before making to cross. She did not notice the thin ice formed from the residue of a light wintery rain shower that had left the ground slippery. One foot on the sleet, and she lost balance. And like a movie in slow motion, she floated in the air, settling in two strong arms that held her firm and helped her to her feet. She turned her head to the person who had given her a hand. Light-blue eyes gazed back. Beside his foot was another cup of coffee lying face down, contents emptied, and in his hand was the same, but now crumpled, brown paper bag with contents safe. This time, he smiled. She, too, smiled, in relief. He noticed she was cold, took off his brown leather jacket, and hung it over her shoulders. She slid into both sleeves, immediately feeling a welcome warmth. Her smile did not fade. 'Thank you for the jacket,' she said, but his smile, like hers, did not fade. *Did he not speak English?*

When he said '*Je m'appelle Florentin*' in an accent that left her bones weak, she wondered what the words meant. Her confusion must have been written on her face because he pointed his right thumb at his chest and said, 'Florentin.'

'Florentin,' she repeated, and he nodded. 'Stella,' she said, and when he repeated it, she also nodded.

They stood awkwardly in silence, looking everywhere but at each other, amusement for the onlookers who could not understand why they stood together, though slightly apart, and facing each other, but not saying anything. When it began to get uncomfortable, like wet socks on feet in tight shoes, she showed him her ticket booklet containing her hotel reservation and program for her three-day stay: Friday to settle in, Saturday for the conference, and Sunday to return home. He barely looked at the program but collected the booklet with his busy hand and picked up her suitcase with his free hand. He gestured with a nod for her to follow, and she did not hesitate.

Abandoning the spilt coffee and overturned cup, he led her on a few minutes walk to a light-blue Peugeot 403 Cabriolet that matched his eyes. He tossed her suitcase and the other things he was holding onto the back seat, right next to some boxes of his own. She looked at them, wondering what his story was, where he was coming from and where he was going. He opened the front passenger's door for her. No questions asked, she hopped in. She did not know where they were headed, but she enjoyed the ride as warm air escaped from the vents and provided comfort. Like mimes, they sat in absolute silence until he fiddled with the radio and settled for a station playing a French song. The vibrato voice of Édith Piaf, who had recently passed away, rang in the lyrics of her popular track, '*Non, je ne regrette rien.*' Although not a single word was understood from the song, she felt a certain sense of freedom move through her as she listened. Her tummy growled again, not too loud and partly clouded by the song but not low enough to go unnoticed. He stretched backwards, retrieved the brown bag, and gave it to her. She took a croissant and dug in, and as the pastry melted in her mouth, the gaping hole in her stomach, caused by hunger pangs, filled up. She relished every bite; it felt like it was her first time tasting it.

Her eyes wandered to the streets, taking in everything she saw and smiling when a sculpture amazed her. From a distance, she saw the *Ponts Couverts*, a set of three bridges and four towers that crossed over the four river channels of River III. He noticed she was excited and made a sudden turn, going off course. He drove through another route where she saw extraordinary monuments, gothic-style structures, and timber-framed buildings, especially in *Petite France*. He found a parking spot, and they continued on foot, walking briskly but prudently because of the cold and the slippery road. They made a first and lengthy stop at the *Cathédrale Notre-Dame de Strasbourg*, where they looked around with loads of tourists who flooded the place, and then at other smaller churches, some of which had been devastated during the war and undergoing reconstruction. They crossed over closed-down tramway tracks and saw other attractions like the *Musée Alsacien*, a museum with over five thousand exhibits, and the historical *Aubette* building that housed a theatre, a gallery, and a café, both of which they did not enter. They walked by the river but hardly spent time there because of how cold she felt.

Even without any tourist information in English, she enjoyed the experience and appreciated the beauty of the medieval cityscape. An experience she would not have thought about or considered were she alone, especially given the weather. She had wished she could visit again in the summer, which had come true, and also thought about all the stories she could tell from just one monument, let alone a city full, which had also become a reality for her.

They proceeded to a bistro where they had a *gratin dauphinois*, a baked potato and cream meal she did not think she would like until she tasted it and could not have enough of it, washed down with local chardonnay. She enjoyed every moment, albeit in accompanied solitude, but it gave her peace. She wished she could remain in the moment forever. As if he had read her mind, when they left the bistro, he retrieved a Polaroid camera from his belongings. She noticed tons of photos stacked together of many places and statues, a tiny proportion of which she had either seen or entered with him. She figured he was a photographer, a journalist, or a mix of both, but definitely in the arts, touring the country or the world and taking pictures. She looked up when she heard him speak French to a man walking by with his arms slightly extended to his sides to maintain balance as he manoeuvred the slippery ground. She now remembered the face of the person who took the photo she had been holding back in Lagos before mysteriously reappearing in Strasbourg.

Probably assuming they were a couple, the man signalled to them to sit on a bollard across the street in front of a *Sogenal* bank with glass doors, her on his lap, but instead, they sat half a bum on it. Their bodies touched, each feeling an inexplicable sensation. They could not wait for the session to be over. The man took his time with the camera. Not able to zoom out fully and capture the artistic background without blurring them, he tried all angles until he gave up and took a haphazard shot after they were no longer able to maintain their smile. The picture came out instantly. The man protected it from the light, then handed it over, along with the camera, and went on his way. They both looked at it, not impressed by their appearance. Not a smile on either face, it seemed as though they were compelled to be there. It did not, however, take away from the memorable moment they had shared.

In the twinkling of an eye, night fell before nighttime, and darkness replaced daylight. She had been amazed the first time, and every other time, she experienced dark winter evenings. It was barely 5 p.m., and the curtains of the sky had drawn close. The street lights and fairy string lights came alive, illuminating and beautifying the city. She smiled, as she had forgotten what it felt like until now. Not done with her yet, he led her by the hand for a nighttime experience. They came to a square in the city centre and were greeted by the statue of Jean-Baptiste Kléber. The inscription under the statue was in French. The only thing she got out of it was the *Général* that preceded the name. She walked by the *Aubette* building from the daytime tour, which had now transformed into a magical edifice with hues of bright light decorating it. People trooped in to view what it held inside.

At the southwest corner of the square named after the general stood an enormous fir tree decorated all over with fairy lights. It looked more magical than real. Scores of people deposited gifts under it, which were collected by the poor and homeless in a surprisingly orderly manner. He led her deeper into the square, to a marketplace that looked like Christmas, from the décor to the clothing of those who manned booths, some selling food, others selling paraphernalia and souvenirs. Fairy lights circled a signpost at the entrance that read *Marché de Noël*. A section of the market was called the *Village du Partage*, with booths only run by charitable organisations for sharing things with the poor and needy. They continued walking around, admiring the scenery, until they stopped at a booth to taste local Alsace delicacies. They first had glazed honey *Bredeles*, bite-size cakes or biscuits made only during Christmas, and then *Bretzels*, the French version of German pretzels, also common in the Alsace region and made from brioche dough.

The next stop was a cheese booth. They perceived the pungent smell even before they saw the booth. He enjoyed a variety of goat's milk cheese; she only tasted a bit and scrunched her face. The final stop was crowded. A booth that sold mulled wine. There were several such booths, and all were packed full. The owners shouted '*vin chaud*' at intervals, heating the red wine in large pots and selling cheap in fancy cups. He bought two and handed her one that warmed her numb fingers. The flavoured steam warmed her cheeks once she brought it to her face, and with the very first sip, she felt as though she had been placed in a soothing sauna, her whole body melting in complete pleasure. She had never tasted anything so sweet and satisfying. She was entranced and wondered how she had forgotten such a moment. She took another sip after another until she emptied the cup. She wanted more. When he offered another cup, she did not refuse. She did not know how many she had had, but she knew she had consumed enough when she began to feel lightheaded and too happy. He led her back to the car.

He drove to the fore of *Hôtel Marguerite*, an Art Nouveau-style building that bore a resemblance to many other monumental structures, and dropped her off by the gate. He alighted and pulled out her suitcase, which a porter took from him. She watched as everything happened in fast-forward motion. She knew nothing about him but did not want him to go. She wanted to spend more time with him. Before she could put her thoughts together, a brief wave of the hand preceded his departure. She mouthed 'thank you' to the air as he entered his car and sped off. Settling into the hotel was relatively easy. They spoke some English and only needed her name to find her a room. She changed into nightclothes, ready to sleep. The night promised protraction and chill, but light-blue-eyed thoughts were going to make it bearable. She wondered if she would ever see him again, at least to thank him properly.

A faint knock at the door cut through her thoughts. She took her time to get out of bed and opened the door to a hand in motion, about to knock again. Light-blue eyes glowed at her. He put his hand down. He still had the same sweater and muffler on. The night had gotten colder, and he had no jacket. She figured he had come back for his jacket. She raised a finger and dashed in, then returned immediately with it. He raised both hands in protest, and she understood he wanted her to keep it. From his back pocket, he pulled out her ticket booklet, which he had forgotten to return to her. She smiled and stretched to collect it. Their hands touched mid-air, and they both froze momentarily. Light-blue eyes pierced deeply into dark-brown eyes. She stepped backwards, and he followed.

Their bodies met in a warm embrace, and lips locked in surrender. As if scripted, his hand found its way under her nightshirt and travelled upwards, climbing from her bikini line to her tummy to her belly button, then between her bosom. She flung her head backwards and let out a shy moan. A kiss rested on her throat, and his hand fondled her fullness, squeezing tenderly, one after the other. She could no longer control herself. She spread her legs, and he lifted her, wrapping her limbs around his waist. The kiss returned with passion as they made for the bed, with clothes skilfully removed and thrown all around the room. Gently, he lay her down, and slowly, he glided into her, awakening sensations she did not know she could have. A first time that felt like magic, her senses heightened and urges aroused by the *vin chaud* that had prepared her for this moment. Each thrust more pleasurable and ecstatic than the last until both climaxed and collapsed into each other's arms.

He did not spend the night. When she held him back to bed, he resisted. She did not understand why he did not want to spend the night with her. She wanted to be with him, forget everything she ever knew and believed in, and run away with him. She did not want to go back to her life in Lagos that had ended the moment their hands touched mid-air and connected. She let him go, hoping that he would return to her like he had done the first time, and together they would build something and learn a common tongue through which their passion would blossom into a romance that would last as long as they lived.

He did not return. Even when she waited all day in her hotel room and missed her conference. He did not return. Even when she stayed up all night and day so that she would hear his faint knock. He did not return. Even when she prepared to leave the hotel, knowing that he had seen her ticket and departure time. He did not return. Exhausted from the mental and physical fatigue, she decided to leave. She opened the ticket booklet and saw the Polaroid they had taken, and her heart sank. It was a definite goodbye before a hello. She flipped it over. There was nothing behind, no goodbye words, not even in a language she would not understand. She shut her eyes as a tear escaped, and when she opened them, boiling heat swathed her. It stung so hard she wondered if she was being pricked by a million needles.

Her eyes adjusted to her surroundings, and the young aspiring writer watched her, sat in the same still position as before her arduous trip down memory lane. Muted ticking took her eyes back to the clock. Barely three seconds had passed since the last time she looked at it. That was all it took for everything to come back to her, the reason she had wanted to forget the story and take the secret to her grave. Now she wished she had not tried to remember. The young writer prompted her again to answer, but how could she tell anyone that the source of her acclaim had been inspired by love that ended before it started, by hope dashed before it materialised, by pleasure that held hands with pain, by honey that left a bitter taste in the mouth? How could she say that she had missed her conference and killed the dream of her parents? How could she reveal that the words the world revered came from a place so adorable yet so deplorable?

She looked at the young aspiring writer and said the same six words she had said over and over to the many who had come before her, and this time, she meant it, 'I'm taking it to the grave.'

THE HEADHUNTER
Desta Haile

'I have told him it's very easy, anyone can fly. All you need is somewhere to go that you can't get any other way. The next thing you know, you're flying among the stars.'
Faith Ringgold

'Everybody all over this planet is always begging the Creator for things, but nobody ever gives the Creator anything. So every morning I give the Creator a song.'
Sun Ra

'I have said it before and I'll say it again— the universe is a gigantic chamber of possibility where everything has the right and chance to happen, and so we must not have cut-and-dry theories regarding just how life should look. Life could surprise us!'
Credo Mutwa

The raucous applause broke the space jazz reverie on which the audience floated so high. Shouts and whoops of appreciation ricocheted off the walls of New Horizons, a tiny legend of a Parisian club. The young musicians' sonic spontaneity soared and dripped off of them in beads of sweat. An eclectic Afropean free jazz riot, The Pyraminds, was taking Europe by storm. A small, low-budget storm, but a storm nonetheless.

They took several bows and received a standing ovation that made the roof tremble. Zerom, the group's trumpetist, made his way humbly through the crowd, through tunnels and bridges of praise, high-fives, fist-bumps, and hugs.

Near the backstage door, an impeccably-dressed older gentleman caught him by the arm.

'The trumpet shakes with great discord,' he said.

'What?'

'Nostradamus, talking about 2023,' the stranger offered.

Zerom couldn't hear anything over the din.

'You play well, my friend,' the man shouted so Zerom could hear him.

'Merci! Are you a musician?'

'Used to be. Drummer.'

'Cool, who did you play with?'

'You wouldn't know them, young man.'

'Try me.'

They entered the backstage area, and the volume eased.

'Sun Ra, Miriam Makeba, Archie Shepp . . .' the man answered.

Zerom's eyes widened as this stranger listed some of his core inspirations. 'No way!'

'You must come see me tomorrow. We will talk music and more.' He gave Zerom a business card that felt like cotton, embossed with his name and address, this random Jean-Claude Point du Sable. 'Come for breakfast,' Jean-Claude instructed before disappearing.

When Zerom managed to slink away to his rented room on the 7th floor of a turn-of-the-century building, he rolled a cigarette and pushed open the skylight with a creak. He put on a record by one of his favourite fellow trumpetists, Hermon Mehari. The blue smoke curled skywards, and he read the card again, mystified by the brief encounter with the old mystery mélomane. Curiosity killed the cat, but sometimes the universe speaks in this strange city, he thought, and music is a universal language. He had a free day before The Pyraminds' European tour continued. He decided he would take up the invitation the next morning.

Immaculately decorated, warmly lit, the place smelled of lilies and luxury. A Faith Ringgold quilt rippled down a wall. A cream-coloured sofa stretched over dunes of sand-tone wood. Black and white photos peppered the wall, monochrome portals each—one of the Sphinx, one of a Black American family finely dressed in their Bronzeville best, and one of a vintage panoramic view of a Caribbean, palm-framed beach with a volcano looming behind it. A wall in the corridor was decked with what looked like a tapestry from an asteroid—dense, mineral.

A beautiful mahogany record shelf boasted loosely-gathered gems from across the ages: Herbie Hancock, Chaka Khan clustered with Ben Lamar Gay in a Chicago corner, Kassav jammed with Jean-Claude Naimro in a Martinique zouk section. Dozens of Sun Ra LPs aligned with kindred spirits like Gary Bartz, Pharoah Sanders, Alice & John Coltrane. The Brazilian section brought Naná Vasconcelos, Itamar Assumpçáo and Hermeto Pascoal in spades, plus Milton Nascimento, Gilberto Gil and Djavan. South Africa was represented by Hugh Masekela, Miriam Makeba, Letta Mbulu, Caiphus Semenya and Ladysmith Black Mambazo.

'This collection is insane,' Zerom blurted in stunned admiration.

Henri Salvador's *Beta Gamma* garbled out of the speakers. Shabaka Hutchings' *Your Queen Is a Reptile* album rested regally against decks.

'So futuristic, so visionary!' Jean-Claude gave an uncle shimmy and finger-snap to the Salvador song. 'This young man from

Cayenne, French Guiana, predicting the future line by line in the 60s: computers, GPS, dating apps—amazing.'

Zerom smiled. 'I like his *Quand Je Monte Chez Toi* best—reminds me of where I stay when I'm in Paris. It is so cheerful that it makes climbing up those endless stairs bearable.'

A low marble table, nestled in the plush surroundings, cradled heavy books on ancient Egyptian mythology, the Haitian Revolution, the Great Migration, Airports, and deep sea creatures. A bizarre but beautiful library. Navajo carpets covered the parquet with geometric cosmology. In the hallway hung indigenous Australian art, myriad dots mapping out Milky Ways of Dreamtime and songlines.

In the adjacent room stood his elaborate desk, decorated with silver-framed portraits of long ago, different worlds, each one containing Jean-Claude at different ages, or JC as he asked to be called. Baby JC, scowling in a tropical yard under a breadfruit tree—the sweet and spicy scent of island twilight faintly palpable. A determined young dude JC on drums, jaw clenched, decked-out in cosmic sapology. An older JC, suited and booted, standing next to a brilliant blue banner for the Movement for the Social Evolution of Black Africa, the man next to him smiling gently at the lens, the woman next to him statuesque in traditional dress and headwrap.

'Barthélemy Boganda. Independence Hero, President of the Central African Republic. My mentor. My guide. And Elisabeth Domitien, the Prime Minister. First woman PM of a sub-Saharan country. Brilliant people. They taught me so much,' JC explained, answering Zerom's unspoken questions in reverse order. 'This photo? Three months we stayed in Egypt. After every gig, Sun Ra would listen to the concert recordings played backwards, over and over again. No drugs, no alcohol. And this, ah, the pearl of the Caribbean—Haiti. Where my father's family is from.'

'Ayiti . . . Point Du Sable—are you related to the founder of

Chicago?'

JC's eyebrows spiked, but he laughed loudly, 'Of course, you know this. And yes, of course, I am. Chicago is an important city for me. You know that's where Sun Ra really became Sun Ra.'

'I thought he was from Alabama?'

'No, maybe born in Alabama, but he was really from Saturn. Chicago is where his music really took root and, how you say, blossomed. Haiti, Chicago, Martinique, Central African Republic—we are one, we come from the same place.'

Zerom took that in with a thoughtful murmur before gesturing to the tiny gold frames dotted on top of a proud grand piano like a mini mountain range. 'And these people? Nice keys, by the way.'

'These people are the three survivors of the Mount Pelée eruption, 1902, Martinique: Ludger Sylbaris, Léon Compère-Léandre, and Havivra Da Ifrile. To remind me that we are survivors, we endure, and we can escape the unimaginable.' He pointed to the name SHADD printed large on the side. 'Black-owned piano company,' he nodded firmly, lips nearly meeting his nose in an expression of profound approval.

Zerom spotted a crystal cabinet brimming with a collection of cigars and fine rums. Plantation XO, Bologne, La Favorite, A1710, Charbonnaud Transat and La Belle Cabresse. One bottle of Togolese sodabi stood out, wrapped in twine and cowrie shells and red wax, stuffed with lemongrass. Goddamn. This guy is not messing around, he said in his head, impressed. 'You should see my wine cellar.' JC smirked as though hearing his thoughts.

The morning bubbled into an exchange of records, songs, and stories, weaving in and out of English, French, and Kreyol like the jazz improvisers both of them were, as if they had known each other for years. The coffee flowed. 'You know in East Africa they drink coffee with rue? Also known as Herb-of-Grace, plant of regret. What do you think they regret then, in Ancient Ethiopia?'

Zerom looked quizzically at his host, who shrugged. 'Your guest is as good as mine,' he said in confident and colourful *franglais*. 'Maybe they regret being sent to Earth for the sins of our forefathers? Maybe they regret taking so much time trying to make it work down here when they could be reclaiming their rightful place as royalty in galaxies beyond?'

'Yeah, so, um, how many languages do you speak, JC?' Zerom sidestepped the weird and winding tangent JC presented.

'Oh, French, Kreyòl, Sangho, *shway-shway* Arabic, a little English. Listen, Z . . . can I call you Z?'

'Anything but Zero.'

'You know, all these fine things, this "expensive shit" to quote Fela, why you think they call them trappings? Because they trap you if you don't know what's going on, man. If you let them brainwash you. When the Black man ruled this land, things were very different. You see, me, I'm the brother of the wind; I am the altered destiny.'

Zerom chuckled but quickly caught himself when he saw JC's face was straight as hell and his eyes were as sombre as coal.

'Okay . . .' Scrambling for a change of subject, he asked his host about a painting on the wall, of a winged serpent-woman frowning and side-eyeing them from a bed of flowers. '*Damballah La Flambeau*, by Haitian artist, Hector Hyppolite. White people see a big red snake with wings, but she is like, big energy, what they call it, The Big Bang?'

'Uh, right. There are snakes on the Martinican flag too, right? Is it connected?' Zerom asked.

'Everything is connected, but that flag is some French bullshit. Fuck the French.' JC was surly again, then shook it off. The storm cloud on his brow smoothed. 'Listen to me, I think your music is incredible, especially your solo stuff, and I want to work with you. Me? I produce, I know people, I want to spread your music all over the worlds. There are just some things you need to understand first.'

A pug waggled into the room with an apologetic smile and wheezed a friendly greeting, his face ridiculously creased, his tail furled tight like a young fern. He sloppily leaned against his master with love that only dogs can deliver. 'Bonjour, Sirius B. You little lazy chops ha!' JC made silly goo-goo faces at his furry friend before snapping back to business.

The next hour spiralled into what felt like a middle school social science class. Laminated maps of Atlantis and the Temple of Mu appeared from who knows where. JC gestured wildly with the fervour of a Ghanaian evangelical pastor, part Neil De Grasse Tyson, part pocket-sized Denzel, spraying Zerom with questions in a thick French accent: 'What's under the Sphinx?' 'Who built the Pyramids?' and 'Quick, come to the window—how many trees do you count in that little park? What shape are they forming?' To Zerom's blank expression, he urged optimistically, 'You see? You see now?' After trying to feign interest for a while, Sirius B the pug made his exit at this point. 'What do you know about Ariel School, Ruwa, Zimbabwe, in 1994? Sixty children being told by aliens that they needed to take care of the environment? Hmm? What! Do! You! Know!'

The crescendo of this intergalactic history lesson was listening to a 15-minute-long symphony written by JC. The song seemed to transcend chronology, and Zerom became increasingly nervous, sneaking a look at his Movado watch to see what time was doing and when he might be able to bounce right out of JC's intense company. The music was wonderful, but Zerom was beginning to question the wisdom of his visit At the end, JC told him, 'This is what I composed . . . for when they return.'

On the way out, JC took him through the garage, where a slate-grey Range Rover rested comfortably. 'Damn, JC,' Zerom whistled, 'did you accumulate all of this through being a jazz drummer?' JC grinned, 'No, my brother, for a long time I was also the financial advisor to the Central African Republic.'

'Aha, I'm in the wrong line of work.' He spotted a shape nestled in the shadows. 'What's that?' Next to the car was something smaller, cloaked in a large blanket of sumptuous velvet. 'Is that your spaceship? Are you going to the moon?' Zerom cracked.

'Why go to the moon?' JC snapped, before he melted into a charming smile. 'There are new horizons you have only dreamt of. Next stop Mars, man, the realm of lightning. Where you wanna go? The door to the cosmos is wide.'

'Ah . . . I'm good, you know. I get bad jet lag.'

'The first time, you will feel a jet lag that you will not believe. Your bones will shout! Whoa! Where is tomorrow, you will ask, ha ha!'

'No, really though, what's under there?'

'My solarship.'

'What does it run on, rum?'

'No, on the intrinsic energies of mythic worlds, you smart ass.'

'Can I see it?'

'No.' JC gave the hidden vehicle a satisfied slap. 'We will travel the spaceways soon enough. The universe sent me to converse with you, to collect those down on the ground, the first guard. The free jazz ambassadors. I'm a recruiter, a headhunter, if you know what I mean, ha!'

He called after Zerom with enthusiasm, 'I meant what I said about your music. It is very special. I will take it to the STARS! Haaa!'

Zerom lay on his bed in his 7th-floor sanctum, feeling somewhat perplexed and blue as the rain dropped steady rowdiness on the skylight. He scrolled through his social media timelines, observing a gloomy, global chain of climate change disasters and Elon Musk's designs on space tourism ('Musk on Mars by 2029!'), bookended by police brutality and more young Black men gunned down like prey. The night before, in a cloud of green haze, Zerom and his Pyramind bandmates had discussed the depressing unlikelihood of racism ever dissipating, at least not in their lifetime. A new, fiercer strain of COVID was spreading, exposing even worse inequality than the first round had. He remembered JC's ranting about looming global obliteration and realised that he maybe wasn't so crazy after all.

Zerom received a text message, not from JC for a change, but from his bank, warning him sternly that he was sinking deeper into his overdraft. The peanuts from the tour were being frittered away with a quickness on expenses, managers, rising rent and the cost of living (the acronym 'COL' made it sound just a touch jazzier). Zerom sighed and threw his phone to the side. What a joke! The Pyraminds were some of the leading jazzmen in the world, but the bottom line still looked like dust. A million streams for what? For who? These streams were forming rivers that gushed into the pockets of the labels, the Spotifies, the whitest 1%—who seemed more and more to make up the majority of their jazz club audiences.

I've Known Rivers by Gary Bartz started to play in his head, and he listened until the pain subsided. He picked up his trumpet and improvised accompaniment, to the music, his permanent companion.

Propping himself up on his side with a sudden start, he thought of the people and places that his kooky but intriguing new friend, JC, had mentioned. He picked up his phone and let his fingers walk through Wikipedia. The more he researched, the more questions he had, and no matter how he diced it, it couldn't be possible that JC had been all the places he said he had unless he was pushing 100 years old. Boganda set up the Movement for the Social Evolution of Black Africa in Bangui in 1949. Sun Ra sailed his Arkestra to Egypt in 1971. And half a century later, JC was here, chatting shit about aliens, looking half his age?

As if on cue, a Whatsapp message popped up from the man himself. It was a link entitled 'The Real Baptism of Christ', which led to a Renaissance-style painting of a UFO blasting the Nativity manger with a golden beam of light. Zerom guffawed and typed 'LOL' but thought better of it and deleted it. Instead he typed, 'Thanks, JC! How you keeping? Any news on the music follow-up you mentioned?'

JC replied, 'Do not worry about that, my friend. I know everybody from Sidney Poitier to Wyclef Jean to Presidents and Prime Ministers. I will take your music FAR FAR FAR!'

Zerom shook his head in exhausted exasperation. 'I'm going to retrain and learn how to code or some shit. This industry is fucking nuts.'

JC continued to show up at gig after gig. Brussels, Glasgow, London, Berlin and beyond. Always alone, always charismatic, always a little strange. Zerom got used to his presence, like an eccentric godfather. Their relationship would cycle between listening to each other's music and the music of the artists they both loved, to JC's obsession with extraterrestrials and the insistence on their imminent return, and to what sounded more and more like hollow promises of helping Zerom get his big break as a stellar trumpeter. Round and round it went, weaving a kind of unusual but inspiring, sometimes infuriating kinship.

However, JC's tall tales were starting to mess with his dreams. Or instigate his dreams, rather, since he never used to dream. His slumber came through swiftly, after smoking, most nights, and he woke feeling a bit crumpled until his first espresso. But now his dreams began to flicker to life, projected on a screen of his sleep. Snippets of JC's ramblings rumbled through the dark: animals gracefully descending to Earth from the constellations that birthed them; Maasai warriors gifted herds of cattle, shuttled through the heavens by a white-bearded god in a metallic canoe; there were fish-people; there were firebirds. 'What the fuuuuck,' Zerom would groan as he woke, making a mental note to get stoned enough at bedtime to retrieve his nocturnal peace. Good sleep, God sleep.

When Zerom complained of this to his garrulous and volatile uncle the next time he saw him, JC quipped, 'The Zulu word for sleep is *butongo*, the state of being one with the star gods. The word for dreams is *ipupo*. The verb "pupa" refers to flight. Therefore to say "I dreamt" means "I flew". A little Credo Mutwa knowledge for your ignorant ass. I guess that means you are almost ready to fly, ha!'

One night, in Istanbul, Zerom smoked on the steep, cobblestone slopes of Galata, near Nardis Jazz Club. He had a bad cold but allowed himself a ritual cigarette before the gig to calm his nerves. JC appeared—which had ceased to surprise his young friend. 'Why are you smoking when you are sick, you idiot? This kind of stupid behaviour is why they exiled us in the first place,' and pointed to the heavens. Zerom closed his eyes and exhaled, silently willing JC to shut up. JC placed a finger on his forehead for a second, and Zerom felt a peculiar, indescribable pulsation. The cigarette dropped out of his mouth, and he stumbled back in surprise, 'What the . . . !' His shock was not so much about JC's antisocial distancing tactics but that the chill that had gripped his sinuses and scratched his throat had entirely disappeared.

'Not so dismissive, now, you little punk, ha,' beamed JC as he bopped smugly towards the entrance. 'Maybe you'll start listening to my old ass!'

He turned around, 'Oh and by the way, I played your music to the head of a really brilliant, uh, label. They want to talk.'

'To me? Or should I take them to my leader?' retorted Zerom, still shaken.

'You are a fool. I should have left you with your snot, *hein*? You might play better, ha!'

Days later, back in his Paris dive for more gigs, Zerom felt totally exhausted. The flights were a mess, and they had lost his suitcase. He got questioned and 'randomly' profiled as usual. Strikes and delays felt like a normal part of travel these days. Life these days. 'New Normal' as if 'Old Normal' was ever normal, or right, or fair. Zerom rolled a spliff and approached the open window, the cool night air embracing him as he puffed. He had a job interview the next day, and he had found some online teaching work in an effort to make ends meet a little less stressfully.

Looking up, his heart nearly stopped. Squadrons of flying saucers formed, shining in glowing flames of emerald-green, blood-red, and copper-yellow against the blackest night. Dozens and dozens of these fiery visitors filled the celestial dome, burning shields in the noiseless night sky. Time froze, stopping the smoke in midair, until a terrifyingly funky bassline unstuck things.

A souped-up, sleek-as-shit kind of badman batmobile hovered three metres from Zerom's open 7th-floor skylight, appearing to be made of solid malachite, with HAVIVRA emblazoned on the side in moonstone tiles. The sound system was insane, blasting the Martinican party tune *Aveou Doudou* so loud that the stars shook. JC was the pilot, dancing in his seat, lit up with maniacal joy. Sirius B's tongue stuck out, and the pug co-pilot's eyes bugged with excitement. JC magically stuck his head straight through the window, which was made of a substance that clearly was not glass, and yelled:

'Are you coming or not, motherfucker?'

THE SISTER-IN-LAW
Jenny Robson

Abide with me, fast falls the eventide . . .

It is the last hymn beginning, thin and scratchy from the speakers. Thin and scratchy like music from Papa's old battery radio before Reagola PowerSurge brought electricity to our homestead.

It is no matter. Only two of us attend, her and me. Well, and also the minister in his dusty suit, closing his dusty Bible on the three verses he read. Still breathing heavy from rushing in late. We, none of us sing even although the words are on the program. With Nigel's picture.

She sits far from me, at the end of the pew. The wife. Well, the ex-wife. With her shoulders bare, even although she is past fifty years, and wearing bright yellow. As if she is a tourist on her first African safari, not here for her husband's cremation. Well, her ex-husband's. Even although she lived in our country seven years, so she must know our customs.

But then also I must be fair. She flew back here from Scotland yesterday. And it is wintertime there, yes? So maybe our heat is too much?

I remember Nigel said, 'Back home, Christmas is snow and warm gloves and cuddling round the fire.'

They come past our town often, the foreign tourists on their African safaris. On their way to our national parks. They sit high in game-drive vehicles, exclaiming in different accents and different languages. They point fingers and cameras at goats by the roadside, at a boy steering an old tyre between two sticks, at a satellite dish on a hut roof. At a migrant Herero woman moving, slow and magnificent in the headdress and clothing of her people.

As they will later point at lion. Or zebra. Or a fresh kill.

But then also, they bring money to our communities. Money and jobs: safari guides, bartenders and cleaners for the lodges. And that is good. Poverty is harsher here in the north than south in the Capital.

The darkness deepens. Lord, with me abide . . .

We sang this at my mother's funeral also. Six years back, at our homestead that lies past the village and fifteen kilometres from town. No speakers there. Only the deep full harmony of aunties and uncles and villagers who held Mama in high respect. We sang also *What a friend we have in Jesus,* that is my mother's favourite. And Pastor Damien read whole chapters from his bible. All those she loved best, God rest her soul.

If my mother was not late, I would not be here in the small chapel with this woman from Scotland. No. Mama would have stopped Desi in her tracks.

'Nyaa, my last-born. You are not a city-girl, giving love to old men for shoes and cell phones. You will tell this Mr McDonald goodbye. Now!'

That would have been the finish of Nigel McDonald and his fat Reagolo salary. And his giant SUV. My mother was tiny but fierce. More so than my father. Even although Papa is six-foot-two. Even although he was a boxer in his young days.

I tried to take Mama's place.

That first time, I am at the gate of our homestead past midnight in my gown and with my hands on my hips. While Desi stumbles with this man past the bougainvillaeas. With his arm round her, pulling her dress open and showing too much young flesh. His SUV is massive like an elephant behind them.

I say, 'Desi, what is this?'

Desi laughs at me. 'This is Nigel,' he says. 'He is Clerk of Works at Reagola. And he is from Scotland.'

'And also he is drunk and old as Papa.'

But Desi pushes past. She leads him across the yard to her sleeping quarters, smelling of beer and perfume.

And what can I do? Papa is away on the lands. My husband is away for a job interview. I tell myself that I will talk to her in the morning. Ask him questions also. Like: where is his wife? Is she back in his home country? And where is his respect to come to our home this way?

I have seen expatriates here these many years, even in our small town. Building shopping malls and fixing infrastructure and studying our animals and digging mines. Always and always well paid because they leave the comfort of their home countries. The excitement glows in their eyes when they first come, for this brave adventure. Even if they squint because the sun is too bright. Maybe the same excitement that the explorers felt long ago. There were pictures of them in our history textbooks before the Department of Education changed the syllabus.

Yes, in the morning I will do my duty. For now, I get my blanket and cross the yard to sleep in the kitchen quarters past the chicken coop.

I do not want to hear.

But next morning, the elephant truck is gone already, with only tracks left in the thick mud. And when I open Desi's door, she is fast asleep with her face innocent and lovely in the morning light. So maybe this was one night's craziness. And now it is done.

I collect the eggs, good-sized eggs today. And I am hoping the interview is good for my husband. But no, Desi's craziness is not done. She stands in the yard, phoning her town friend. Loudly.

'Oa, stop it, Pinkie. I'm telling you: he loves me—he said it like ten times. Hah, who cares? The wife, she is safe in the Capital. In her fancy house.'

I don't like Pinkie. She is a town girl with a town girl's habits. I worry that Desi spends time with her, staying many nights in her room above Nando's. Pastor Damien tells us from the Bible, from Matthew, 'Judge not, that ye be not judged.' He says it often, and his voice booms out across the village and into the bush. Speaking in our language often. But still, I worry.

'Oa, and listen to this, girlfriend. He's taking me to a safari lodge. He promised. Four star, maybe five!'

Then she packs some things and leaves, walking to the village where she can hitch a ride back to town.

And my husband returns at sunset. Still jobless.

Swift to its close ebbs out life's little day . . .
The ex-wife stares at the coffin on its trolley behind the open curtains. Dusty maroon curtains. She has not looked at me, not one time. Maybe she thinks I am part of the crematorium staff?

When Nigel died, I phoned her where she lives in Motherwell in Scotland. To tell her the arrangements. I used Nigel's phone because my airtime was finished. But I didn't understand what she said back. Her accent was confusing, and her shouting was loud. Maybe from shock? Or maybe she thought I was Desi?

*

The elephant SUV is back after some few weeks. And it is Desi driving. Desi—when she doesn't have a licence! She slides down from the driver's side, wearing new clothes. Her high heels sink in the sand, so she clings to Nigel's arm. He carries a blue cooler box, and I hear ice and bottles inside.

'Where have you been?' I demand. 'Why didn't you answer your phone?'

She pouts at me with lips glistening from gloss. My husband comes from the woodpile with his axe.

Desi introduces. 'This is my boyfriend, Nigel. And this is my brother-in-law, Thata.'

Boyfriend? When he is past fifty years? But my husband drops his axe and shakes hands. As if all is fine and right. And the two men sit outside on our white plastic chairs under the marula tree. The shade is good there. My grandfather planted that tree before my father was born even.

They drink beers from Nigel's blue box while Desi and I prepare food. They discuss like all men discuss—about the rains, about the bad accident on the highway last weekend, about a corrupt politician who hanged himself in his garage before the police came, about an old male elephant attacking farms in the northeast.

But I see how his eyes follow my sister all the while. Almost I drop the bowl of morogo into the sand. His eyes are wrinkled and bloodshot and very blue. Bluer even than Pastor Damien's. I tell myself this will not last. Desi changes boyfriends often. She will get bored soon of this old man.

It doesn't help.

Desi sits down on his knee so that the chair legs bend over. His free arm winds around her bare waist like a python. Scaly and too too red.

Sometimes I worry for these expatriates, for how our fiery sun damages their skin. Even their factor sunscreen is not strong enough to protect. And their minds too, maybe, when they are not used to daily day-long heat.

My husband says that is nonsense. He says overseas, sometimes they have hot summers. Sometimes they get heat waves.

I say, 'Mr McDonald, you must put ointment on your arms. And your neck also. I have if you want.'

He says, 'Call me Nigel, Boka. And dinna stress. A wee bit of sunburn never hurt anyone.'

Desi giggles and tells us that 'wee' is Scottish for little.

Earth's joy grow dim, its glories pass away . . .

She breaks down sobbing suddenly so that her shoulders shake. Does she still call herself Mrs McDonald?

I know she went back to Scotland before the divorce even. As soon as she heard the stories. Back to her two grown daughters in Motherwell.

They were angry, the daughters. They refused to speak to him ever. Not even on Christmas Day, when the whole world forgives, to honour the birthday of Baby Lord Jesus. Are they angry still, or do they regret now that their father is late?

And Mrs McDonald? Does she love him still? Even although he brought her pain? Her sobs are heartbreaking. I want to slide down the pew to wrap my arms around her and rock away the grief. To rub her heart that is hurting.

But I don't move. Neither the Minister.

We are finishing the meal when Desi's phone rings. She jumps off Nigel's lap and runs to the bougainvillaeas. It is her friend Pinkie. Desi speaks in our language, so the legoa won't understand.

'Of course he's still my boyfriend. What do you think?'

Boyfriend? We have a word in our language for such men as he is. An ugly word. And a word also for girls who run with such men.

It is an even uglier word, and I don't want to think about Desi in that way.

'And listen to this, chick. He promised to buy me a car. Imagine! Then we can hit the city lights, girlfriend. You and me only!'

Or maybe he does understand? Some expatriates try to learn our language, even if they complain it is tricky. When I was a girl, coming from school with my friend Tsholo, we saw a Teach Yourself book for expatriates in the bookstore window. It had lists of sentences: Wash this. Clean that. Sweep this. Plant that.

We giggled, Tsholo and me, saying the sentences in our silliest accents.

'Thatshwa diaparo.'

'Kgaola bojang.'

Until the bookstore owner chased us away. I do not think such books get sold now. It was long ago and a different time.

But Nigel and my husband are discussing again. And now it is the job interview. My husband spreads his hands out wide, and it hurts in my heart to see he feels hopeless. He had a good job once, and we lived in a town in the central district. In a second-floor flat with a balcony. But then the company closed. And we came back here to the homestead and my parents.

Nigel opens more beers and leans forward.

He says, 'Listen, Thata, mate, no decent, hardworking man should be unemployed. That's not on. Let me have a chat with my big boss, aye?' Then he picks up the empty cooler box and calls Desi, still drinking his beer.

'Off we go, ma bonny lass.'

She giggles. 'That means my beautiful girl,' she tells us.

And Thata and I wait impatiently. By Friday, I phone Desi.

'Will you and Nigel come this weekend? Papa is back from the lands.'

'Oa! And now suddenly you like my boyfriend, is it?' she mocks me.

And yes, I admit: I am not blameless in all this that happened. Desi, she gets her car, a silver BMW. It is secondhand, but she is happy. And my husband, he gets an interview appointment with Nigel's big boss. So he is happy.

Papa is not happy. He shakes hands with Nigel, courteous always, no matter how things are. But then he goes to his quarters, saying that he is tired after the land clearing. He closes his door against us.

Change and decay in all around I see . . .

A sudden wind comes through the window, lifting the curtains. Lifting the petals on the white wreath. Mma Lecoge from the village made it for two trays of eggs. There is no wreath from the ex-wife.

Yet she is sobbing still. Maybe she finds it in her heart to forgive him now? After all the gossip and the hurt and the loss?

My aunties arrive at the homestead, climbing out of a small Corolla taxi. They wear traditional dresses and shawls to show this visit is serious. I know well why they are here. Gossip moves like a dry-season bushfire in our communities, as it does in the expatriate community.

And Papa knows also. He greets the aunties courteously, bending low because they are all three tiny like my mother. He apologises that he must leave—it is church choir practice in the village, and he cannot miss it. He does not look at me. Because choir practice is on Friday mornings only, and right now it is Tuesday afternoon.

My aunties refuse the plastic chairs. So I lay out mats on the sand against the wall. When they are settled with mugs of Rooibos tea, it begins.

'So where is your sister? We hear bad things—'

'Very bad things, Bokamoso. That she is running with this legoa, this old and married legoa. Staying with him in hotels—'

'Ee, my neighbour's son, he works at the Holiday Inn. She was in this man's bedroom. In this man's bed when he brought the room-service breakfast—'

'It is a shame and a disgrace to our family—'

I nod my head respectfully. Over and over. I promise I will talk to Desi when she is home again.

'This is your duty now your mother is late, God give her eternal peace. And your father, he is too soft . . .'

At last, at last, when the sun is low, the Corolla taxi comes back to collect them. Papa appears again from the thick bush where he waited.

But Desi stays away that night. She declines when I phone. Papa and my Thata sit into the late hours, talking around a small fire. They are both quiet men. It is what bonds them. But I can hear from the open door of my bedroom now the wind has died away in the marula leaves.

'Soutpiel,' says my father.

'Rra?'

'When I was young and working in the mines in South Africa, that is what the Boers called the English contract workers. Soutpiel. It means salt prick.'

'Why, Rra?'

'It is because the contract worker, he stands with one leg in his home country and one leg in Africa. So that his bonna dangles in the ocean water. Getting salty, you understand?'

'Ee, Rra.'

My father sighs a heavy sigh. 'In the end, they don't know which place they belong. So they are lost. And with nowhere that is home for them. It is so with this man Nigel. I see this in his eyes. And I am sad for my princess to be with a man who is lost.'

*

Desi and Nigel come some few days later, in the shiny secondhand silver BMW. I say nothing about the aunties' angry instructions. Nor my father's sadness. And why not? Because my sister will not listen. Desi wants what Desi wants. I know this. From when she was small, she was stubborn and strong-willed as a village donkey. She used to stand solid and refusing, and with her fists defiant on her hips, yelling, 'Nyaa, nyaa!' My father looked down at her, smiling and shaking his head. Sometimes laughing out loud at his last-born, his little Princess Desi. Even although my mother scolded them both.

And yes, I confess this: also because we are waiting to know about the job. Thata's interview was four days back.

Desi's eyes are glowing with happiness. 'Do you see my car? Isn't it awesome, Boka? And Nigel has something for Thata.'

What Nigel has is an envelope. Inside, the letter reads, *Dear Mr Ndwapi, Reagola PowerSurge is pleased to inform you . . .*

So Thata's eyes glow now also. Even my father comes from his room to congratulate my husband and to thank Nigel. And Nigel fetches a bottle of special Scottish whiskey from the silver car. Glenlivet, it is called. I have a small glass and my father and Thata also. Nigel and Desi have many glasses after my father has gone to bed.

It is October now, our hottest month. Thata is fixed and happy in his job. Each morning he wears a smart shirt and goes with the taxi he booked into town.

He says, 'Maybe soon I will get a raise. My foreman says my work is good and steady. Maybe soon, Boka, we can get a flat in town?'

I wave when the taxi drives off in the dust.

But I do not want to leave the homestead. Even if it is not a comfortable place and sandy. And with no satellite TV and no air conditioner and no wifi like they have in town. And with only outside taps for washing. And the toilet outside also. And with snakes and scorpions coming into the yard sometimes.

Papa is here. And my chickens that are laying well. And the quiet of the bush is a peaceful thing around me.

Desi and Nigel come to visit. In the giant SUV because Desi's car is at the garage with some dents where she hit a pole. A Reagola pole! She still does not have a licence.

She joins me in the coop, where I am scattering maize. I have not seen her in a long time. Nor spoken with her. She tries not to step on the chicken kaka. Nigel and Thata are in the plastic chairs, discussing their jobs. And Papa is back on the lands because his strongest ox is sick.

She says, 'And guess what, Boka? The best news ever. You will never guess!'

'What?'

'The divorce is done. Nigel is free.'

'Free?'

'Free for us to marry. He promised he will get a ring. A real diamond engagement ring.'

She talks on and on and fast while the hens cluck and fuss by her feet. They will move into the posh house in the Capital. And she will throw out all the ex-wife's furniture and buy new. And Pinkie will stay with them. There is a guest room next to the swimming pool.

I struggle to breathe. Twice, thrice I try. And then the words rush out my mouth, and I cannot stop them.

'Are you crazy? You don't love him, Desi. You only love his money. You only love the things he buys.' And I use the word, God forgive me! The ugly ugly word for such a girl. 'That's what you are, Desi!'

She slams the chicken-wire door against me. She shouts, 'And you, Bokamoso, you are judgmental. Always judgmental. Even Pinkie, she says so. Who are you that you can judge everyone?'

She sits with the men and cleans the kaka off her shoes with a tissue.

Thata is calling for me to join them round the small fire. Even in the hottest months, a night fire is a comfort and friendly. But I say I have a headache and I must lie down. Late into the night, I hear Desi still giggling, teasing Nigel for the bald patch on his head.

But the hurt in my heart and in my mind don't stop. Because my sister called me judgmental. And she is right. And how can that be—when I try so hard to walk in the shoes of others? When I try so hard to understand how they see the world?

'Are you feeling better this morning, Boka?'

Nigel stands at the door to the kitchen quarters. I am stirring mabela into boiled water. He smells of toothpaste and men's deodorant so that the smell is all around me.

He says, 'Boka, I need your help. You need to tell me how to do everything the right way.'

'For what?'

My stirring is too rough. My hand on the spoon is too tight, so brown porridge slops over onto my clean red tablecloth.

'To marry your sister, aye,' he says. 'Just think, Boka: You will be my sister-in-law.'

He tries to help clean the mess. But he makes it worse.

Hold Thou Thy cross before my closing eyes . . .

The minister taps his fingers on the pulpit. It is a long hymn, this one, with many verses. Beside him, a thin rope dangles against the wall. I think it is the rope he must pull to close the curtains.

Outside in the street, the noise is growing. Cars hooting rhythms, people shouting across to one another, car radios playing songs with the bass booming and shaking the air. Everyone is preparing for New Year's Eve.

Nigel and Desi walk to the hill by our homestead to watch the sunset. They walk hand-in-hand, and I can see their body shapes against the red and bright orange sky. She puts her head on his shoulder. He keeps his arm around her and whispers close to her ear.

Our sunsets are famous. Magnificent colours, every and every evening. My husband says it's just the sand and dust in the air.

And maybe? Maybe I am wrong, and Nigel and Desi are in true love? And right for each other? Maybe they can be happy, and their life together can be good? Who can explain why we love the person we love? There were some who questioned when Thata and I married. And look now.

But in the end, Nigel and Desi did not marry. In the end, Nigel got fired.

Late November and Papa's choir is busy with carols. Four days a week. When the wind is right, the harmonies travel across the bush to our homestead. *Silent Night, Holy Night.* Or *Loseanyana,* my favourite.

My husband comes home to tell me.

'It is a terrible thing, Boka,' he says while the taxi is U-turning back to town. 'Drunk on duty. That's what the big boss said. He hit the wrong switch, and now two workers are in hospital. One of them maybe will die.'

'Desi? Does she know?'

My husband shrugs and goes to wash. I try to phone Desi, but she declines. Later she texts: *On my way to da City with Pinks. Dis silver baby is da bomb.*

I leave a voice message: 'Drive carefully. Come home soon.' The roads are dangerous for speeding and accidents. Especially the highway to the Capital. Especially in holiday times.

But two weeks before Christmas, Desi is still gone. Maybe she knows? I confess: I am thinking—hoping, yes hoping—that this will be the end of marriage talk. Even although she has her diamond ring.

And it is Nigel who comes to our gate. With no SUV and no taxi. Maybe he walked all the fifteen kilometres? He looks dusty and tired, and his backpack is heavy.

'Thata, Boka? Can I stay here, just a wee while? Just till this so-called Season of Goodwill is over, and I can find a new job?'

He has run out of money, he explains. He gave his wife most of their savings and the money from the house sale also. And Desi has taken his credit cards.

'So I am royally screwed,' he says. 'Aye, up shit's creek without a paddle.'

And how can we refuse?

'I won't get in the way, promise. I'll keep to myself.'

And he does. Most days he sits in a plastic chair and stares at the bush. In the distance, there are the Reagola power lines he helped to fix. Long hours he sits, drinking beer if he has. I think my husband brings him when I am not looking. Papa ignores him. But Papa is mostly at the village with the choir. I have given up phoning Desi. Even Pinkie won't answer my calls.

Sometimes Nigel helps me collect and sort the eggs. Sometimes he delivers trays to the village. Early mornings he washes his shirt from yesterday at the tap and then stands with me to wave Thata goodbye.

I hear him on his phone, there in Desi's room. His voice is

desperate and pleading.

'Please, love. Send the bucks so I can get to you. Just give me one more chance. Dinna throw away all we had. I swear I won't let you down a second time. You are all I have left in this world, my bonnie lassie . . .'

And is he talking to Desi? Or to his wife?

'Aye, I know. I lost my mind, I reckon. Craziness and sunstroke and long hours and too much booze.'

It is the wife, I think. And how does he dare to call my sister craziness and sunstroke?

'Well then, at least, talk to Steffi and Chrissie for me. Ask them to take my calls. It's been seven months.'

Christmas morning, and Desi is still not home. And still declining. I am in my new pink suit and hat for the Christmas Service, and Thata is smart in his new jacket, even although he will get hot later. Already Papa and the choir have begun their carols. The wind is blowing from the village, so we hear.

'Come with,' I invite Nigel. 'It is not right to be alone Christmas Day. You can borrow Thata's other tie.'

'Maybe later,' he says. 'I must try phone my girls again. Christmas was magic when they were little. Surely they must remember? Aye, we had such fun. Especially when it snowed. I bought them new gloves every year, bright furry gloves. And then we would cuddle up in front of the fire while their Mam cooked. Good, good times.'

He is smiling as he waves goodbye. But his lips are trembling. And also the phone in his hand.

Heaven's morning breaks and earth's vain shadows flee . . .

It is the last verse now.

Desi promised she would come to the service. But when I phoned last night, Pinkie answered.

'She's not here, Boka. She's out with this rich Canadian guy. And tomorrow night we're off to a New Year party at Ceasar's.'

Desi is young still. Maybe she is learning her life lessons? Maybe someday she will find her balance and choose wisely? I hope.

The minister tugs at the rope. Tugs a second time, more roughly, and the curtains slowly join together. The coffin is gone from our sight. It is the sign and the signal that Nigel belongs no more in this world. Not in Scotland, not in Africa.

The minister pats Mrs McDonald's shoulder. 'Deepest condolences, Mma. I am sorry for your loss. May your husband's soul rest in eternal peace.'

'Ex-husband's,' she corrects.

He walks across to me. 'And you are?'

What can I say? That I am Nigel's sister-in-law? Well, his almost-sister-in-law?

'A friend.'

In life, in death, oh Lord, abide with me . . .

The speaker shuts off suddenly, leaving the last chord hanging in the air, thin and scratchy and unfinished.

She stands in front of me in her sleeveless yellow dress and with her face hard, as if I am the enemy. And yes, maybe in her eyes, I am. I am part of this place that brought destruction to her family.

'I am taking his ashes back to Scotland,' she says, as if I will argue.

The carols are ringing in my ears still, comforting and joyous. We walk back from the village, hand-in-hand, my Thata and me. Papa follows with Pastor Damien beside him, two tall and dignified elders.

But at the gate, by the bougainvillaeas, I stop and stare. Confused.

Papa's rope that he uses for his oxen is up in the marula tree. Tied around a thick branch. And down on the ground, a white plastic chair lies on its side. And between the rope and the chair, between the marula leaves and the yard sand, Nigel's body hangs.

I cannot move. Thata and Pastor Damien rush forward—as if it is not already too late. And my father, my quiet and courteous father, screams with rage. More angry than I ever in my life saw him before.

'Filthy dog with no respect! How dare you defile our home? With no thought for the people who welcomed you in. Coward! Running away instead of facing your sins and your punishments like a man.'

Nigel's body is on the ground now. Thata is phoning the police. And I am moving at last, going to our sleeping quarters for a blanket. So that I can cover Nigel's face. His face has become something from a nightmare.

Pastor Damien puts his hand on my father's shoulder that is still shaking with his anger.

'Judge not, my brother.'

Pastor Damien's eyes are calm and kind, even with all this. I think maybe he is a man who has the whole world for his home. Mama admired him greatly; God rest her soul.

And God rest the soul of this poor lost man under my blanket.

THE HYENA AND THE TWO-HEADED GOAT
Alex Kadiri

Although both men must have come to Workers Village around the same time, no one paid Agaba any mind. He was mostly unremarkable: tall, spoke very fast, snorted snuff. Agogo-Igbala wasn't so lucky. He possessed distinguishing features, features that called attention to him like flies to shit. And this was before we learned of his gift. His real name was Boga. No one knew what it meant, but a man's name is his name, so we called him just that until it shrunk and became too small to contain the man that he was.

If we went by physique, Boga was just the perfect name—short. The man was exactly like that. A few inches shorter, he'd have crossed the line into dwarfism. He was 5'1 at best, bent over, and carried a hump bigger than a camel's on his back. This load seemed too much for a man of such small frame, but Boga carried it well, showing no signs of exertion except for the small limp in his right leg.

I was twelve when Boga first came, the daughter of two schoolteachers. He arrived in a lopsided moving van that stopped across the road, right outside the Uzohos' old house, which should have been identical to ours, except the Uzohos had painted a dull layer of beige over the initial mud-brown coating. Because the beige was too thin, the brown peered out from underneath like skin through see-through fabric. This gave the walls a tawdry finish. I watched the driver empty the van, working quickly as if he had to beat traffic, then Boga as he struggled to move the unloaded bags and furniture into the house.

Boga came just before dusk, right as daylight waned and chickens returned home to roost. Maybe it was the distance from where he'd set out. Maybe he just preferred the faint cover of twilight. Whatever it was, it was the first thing I saw once he stepped out of the vehicle—the hunch on his back. Even in the failing light, it was a hard thing to miss. The way his back curved upwards so it looked like he carried an anthill under his slackened, stretched-taut T-shirt. The way his neck sank between his sloped shoulders so it appeared he had none. The man looked deformed, like poorly moulded playdough, like he was God's attempt at a cruel joke.

I sat on the concrete landing of our stoop biting the kernels off my half-eaten corn, which was sugar-sweet but boiled too soft. I noticed the appetite die in my stomach, the taste vanish from my mouth as I watched this strangely built man. Perhaps from repulsion or a lack of concentration, it wasn't long before the corn slipped out of my hand and rolled along in the dirt, gathering grit. One quick glance at it, and I was back staring at Boga. It took every ounce of my composure to keep a straight face, to not dash inside screaming for Biggie so he'd come outside and see what I saw, that a hunchback was going to be our new neighbour. The hunchbacks I knew sat in the scorching Lokoja sun every day, roasting away as they sang nasal songs and panhandled along Ganaja and Felele, and so this made no sense.

One year younger than me, Biggie was my brother; his birth name was Socrates because my father hoped he'd grow to become a scholar. When he filled out into a plump round kid, everyone called him Biggie, and the name stuck and remained even after he'd shed the baby fat. I studied Boga closely, in the way I'd never studied for an exam, but all I saw on that first day as the darkness congealed around us was the hunch. Not the man. Not the colour of his shirt. Just the hunch.

Even though his belongings didn't look like much, not everything made it indoors that night, and on the second day, a Saturday, when he came out at the ass crack of dawn to clear the rest, it was the commotion of clanging kitchenware, the wailing of heavy furniture, and the frustrated hissing of a man trying, and failing, to be discreet that forced me awake. Eyes crusty from sleep, I made my way to the living room window. Biggie came with me. Together we peered out at Boga. In the weak light of dawn, Boga resembled the crafty goblins in my old storybooks. I told Biggie this, and we giggled. We remained there for another fifteen minutes until the semi-darkness outside thinned to daylight. That was when I saw his face for the first time: the hollow eyes beneath jutting brow ridges, high-domed Cro-Magnon forehead, lips set in tired lines. It was the face of sadness, of disillusionment. In that face, I saw a man enduring the worst kind of grief.

Boga seemed like the kind of person who'd suffered a recent tragedy. He hung his head low, slouched his already-slouched shoulders, and carried himself with a defeated aura. When he moved, his motions were uninspired, zombie-like. He didn't even crack a smile when Old Soldier bellied up to him—gut exposed like a hairy calabash, shirt hanging limply from a shoulder—and welcomed him to the neighbourhood in that robust voice of his. His response seemed hurried, perfunctory, like Old Soldier was a Jehovah's Witness come to peddle nuisance and the good news. And when he'd carried in the last of the items—an ugly hardwood desk and chair—he didn't resurface for another week.

*

Workers Village wasn't really a village. It was a housing complex, a small community of identical and almost-identical houses separated by neglected bougainvillaea shrubs, of families so cordial each constantly minded the other's business. It was marked by lichened walls and decrepit driveways, squeaky gates and dying lawns. A couple of fruit-bearing trees stood beside houses where the occupants hadn't axed them down. Sometimes the lazy breeze borrowed the smells of their issues—the rotten-sweet odour of decomposing cashew, the sweet-sour smell of overripe bird-damaged mango, the citrus scent of lime. Other times it carried the suffocating smell of swine, the hard-hitting stench of cow dung or goat droppings or fermenting cassava. Hemmed in from behind by rocky mountains and evergreens, the fences were an exhibition of tattered election posters and church flyers, and the grounds crawled with untended livestock, all of them as unregenerate, as uncompromising as hardened criminals. Workers Village was a world of its own.

Afternoons in Workers Village were coloured with heat and noise. Children sang their hearts out as they hopped off school buses. Adults fraternized under the shade of surviving trees, parakeets chirruping above as the men, their bodies slippery with sweat, broke and nibbled on kola nuts, all the while swapping work tales because the heat inside was belligerent. A few people circled their houses in search of a broken pipe or dislodged louvre that needed fixing. Some others stopped for long minutes along the road to say 'agba' – 'naago'—in that back-and-forth way tennis balls travel—when they came across a familiar face. The Igalas greeted this way, repeating the words and saying little else until one or both was saved by the bell or drifted thankfully out of earshot.

On languorous afternoons like this, Agaba sat by himself outside his house in a dilapidated, largely vacant block. Often, he was shirtless and had a noisy radio with a long, crooked antenna balanced on the wobbly plastic table right beside the glass snuff bottle. Agaba wasn't given to fraternizing as much as the other men of the estate. Quite frankly, I'd never seen him sit in conversation with another man except for Old Soldier, who made it his business to be in everyone's business, who it was said had felled many men in his hay days fighting in the army, and who didn't pass up an opportunity to recount tales of the same.

Like Boga, Agaba was a fresh arrival, but he'd been here at least a month longer, having arrived around Easter. He'd joined us only two weeks before I started to notice some absurdities, like his eyes following me when I strolled by on an errand, even though I was prepubescent and still built like a boy. Or his fly habitually left undone so that his manhood stuck out, iron-hard, sometimes nodding like a lizard, a crooked smile plastered on his face. On the few occasions when he wasn't outside, I'd notice the variegated curtain part lightly in his living room, just enough to permit the perp a decent line of sight. Agaba never said much, only listened, only grunted in response when I greeted. But his eyes, they made me feel naked, violated, as microorganisms must under a microscope.

By the second week, after Boga began to come out because he'd somehow found work in a sawmill, he learned that the children of the estate were not in the habit of guarding their gazes, or their tongues or expressions. Everywhere he went, children paused to stare at him as though he were a magic trick, as though he were a creature from outer space. Boga didn't seem to like this very much. But there wasn't much he could do about it. Toddlers bolted on feeble bowed legs when they saw him. Bigger kids cast overt glances punctuated with cheeky side comments and mischievous grins. A few adults who'd begun to notice him or who'd overheard their children's excited chatter about the 'hunchback who eats children' threw sidelong glances. One or two even slowed their overheating jalopies to say 'hi' or engage him in quick interrogations disguised as conversations.

'You're new to our estate?'

'Yes.'

'When did you move in?'

'Last week.'

'Ah, welcome eh, welcome. So what do you do?' And as an afterthought, 'If I may ask.'

'I work at the sawmill near Felele market.'

'Sawmill? Isn't that dangerous work? What does your wife say about it?'

'I'm not married.'

'You can't be serious. You're not?'

'No.'

'I won't even ask why.' A pause. An exaggerated smile. 'But you have children?'

A delicate almost-impatient shake of the head.

'Too bad. What did you say your name was?'

'Boga.'

'Ah, yes. That is it. Boga. Solid name. You're Yoruba, right?'

A small nod. 'Yes.'

'Good. Good. How are you liking this place so far?'

A so-so shrug.

It wasn't long until Boga retreated into his shell, adjusting his schedule so that he left and returned at odd hours when hardly anyone remained outside to see him. But then the heatwave came, so stifling fans blew hot breeze and pores leaked like faucets. Soon, chickens began to run around in circles, their necks twisted and hanging to the side. Dogs staggered drunkenly until they keeled over and lost consciousness. Pigs collapsed like it was a competition. The owners, complete ignoramuses in animal care, ran around frantic, sweating, palms fanning themselves as they asked questions whose answers stared them right in the palm, or screamed bird-flu, swine-flu, dog-flu.

Around this time, Biggie's disposition toward Boga began to change. Or maybe it had always been like that. He didn't let free his roaring laugh when I wisecracked about Boga's hunch resembling the mountain behind our estate or his big forehead bearing striking semblance to our grinding stone. Each carefully thought-out joke fell flat, like stale, iron-pressed rubbish. And then, one evening, I found out why. I came outside calling for him, perambulating as I did, my pitch rising with each prolonged yell. Silence called back. Just when I'd given up and turned to go back inside, I caught sight of him across the road, a blur of cocoa-coloured skin, khaki-brown school shorts and white fishnet singlet, half of him hidden from plain view by the stuccoed walls making up Boga's home. They were in the backyard, talking, laughing, the same boy who no longer laughed at my jokes. I knew it then: Biggie was connecting with Boga in ways no one else did.

Incensed at this spectacle, I marched to the middle of the road, summoned all the power within my twelve-year-old body and packed it into that next yell. Biggie heard this time. He strode over and glared at me, darts in his eyes, daggers in mine.

'What?'

'Mummy said you should come and remove your stinking shoes from the parlour.'

When I finally forgave Biggie the next day because he was my only sibling and because the only thing harder than holding a grudge at twelve is remembering to hold it, he told me all about their friendship.

'He's very good with animals. The other day, I was playing fetch with Mrs Lawani's dog, and it just lay down and started breathing slow like it was going to die. Boga saw us. He asked me to bring the dog. I left it with him, and when I returned like five minutes later, Master was jumping around again.'

I squinted in confusion. Was Biggie saying he was a vet? I asked this, and he shook his head.

'So what did he do?'

'I don't know.

'Maybe Master was just pretending?'

Biggie shook his head, disagreeing. 'Yesterday, before you called me, it was that Mr Yaro's agwagwa with those fat bumps on its face and legs. I saw it lying upside down. It looked dead. I wasn't even sure Boga could do anything, but I decided to try. When I brought him the duck, it woke up and ran off.'

'And you didn't see what he did?'

'No. He asked me to wait outside.'

Boga resuscitated more animals over the next few weeks, some brought to him by the owners because they'd caught wind of his activities and wanted to see for themselves. More than anything, they wanted to know how this pariah restored life to dying things. But no one saw anything. Boga wouldn't allow any witnesses when he administered his magic. Soon the rumours grew wild and spread like an epidemic.

'A wizard, perhaps?'

'No, a businessman who doesn't want to disclose the tricks of his trade.'

'But he's not charging anything for it.'

'He will, soon. Nothing is free.'

'Herbs then?'

'Yes, must be herbs and concoctions.'

Boga explained to them that they had to keep their animals watered and shaded, maybe lay a tarp over their goat pens and pigsties, have the animals confined within, anything to protect them from the blazing sun. Educated fools that they were, they listened and nodded, but when they went away, they maintained it was a new kind of flu. What did Boga know? The sun in previous years had been just as unforgiving. And so, they kept to their old system and continued bringing him their dying animals. By reason of these events, the people of Workers' Village grew to be more accepting of him. They invited him to sit with them, and as Boga began to honour these invitations, as they broke kola nuts with him and showered him with praises, so did the christening begin to take root.

Tunbosun was the first one to call him Agogo-Igbala. He was the estate barber and, like Boga, was Yoruba. He told everyone that the name roughly meant 'bell of salvation'; it was how healers were addressed in his hometown. They all agreed it was a good fit. Before long, no one remembered he was 'Boga' anymore. To them he was now Agogo-Igbala, healer of pets and livestock.

When they inquired about his origin, Agogo-Igbala explained he was from Kwara State, where hunchbacks were currently being abducted, their humps harvested for money rituals. Worse still, he hailed from Omu-Aran, a backwoods community where corpses of his ilk weren't buried but hung from trees to ward off unnecessary evil. His uncle, who lived here in Lokoja, had found him this accommodation and gotten him the sawmill job because he believed these were 'saner climes'. The men nodded in agreement and expressed their shock at the level of barbarism still happening in the world.

Gradually, Agogo-Igbala began to readjust his arrival and departure times because the hostility had gone from people's brows. They now saw him as one of them, welcomed him into their midst without prejudice, engaged him in quick games of draughts. And as they did this, they began to see that underneath the defective exterior, the introversion, Agogo-Igbala had a phenomenal mind. He saw things they didn't, said Einstein-smart things, beat them at their own games.

But breaking bread with the adults didn't guarantee a breakthrough with the children. Fingers still pointed when he limped past, tongues still wagged. Only, this time, he had the support of Biggie. On one such occasion, a boy playing *monkey post* football stopped along with some of the other boys and cough-shouted 'aneje' because tortoises carried humps on their backs too. At once, Biggie flashed the boy a dirty look.

'Shut up! Have you seen the size of your ear?'

Another boy burst out laughing. 'Wide like a hand fan.'

And then everyone was chanting 'hand fan ear' until the boy hid his embarrassment behind a foolish smile and ambled off quietly to nurse his wounded pride.

As the boys resumed their game, kicking around a *felele* ball on the dusty tarmac, I saw the warmth enter Agogo-Igbala's eyes. I saw the ghost of a smile flicker across his face. I saw the unspoken appreciation behind his lips. What I didn't see was the new frailty that now tainted his walk, the small almost-imperceptible gauntness that sharpened his edges, that bit by bit, something appeared to be taking a toll on him.

Independence Day 2010, a Friday, the day news of two car bombs going off simultaneously in Abuja flooded the TV stations, I woke with a start. When I tried to recall the dream I'd been having, all that came back was a hyena and a two-headed goat. I couldn't make sense of it. Later that evening, I heard my mother call out my name from the living room.

'Where's your brother?' she asked.

'I don't know.'

'What do you mean you don't know?'

Unsure how to respond, I stayed mute.

'Look at the clock. What's the time?'

I stared at the minimalist wall clock to the far right. 'Quarter to six.'

'Quarter to six, and common sense hasn't told your brother to come home.'

Silence.

My father turned from the news. 'Where did he even say he was going?'

The question was directed to my mother, but she turned and planted her gaze on me, effectively redirecting it. 'He didn't tell me,' I said, unsure to whom I was responding.

My father hissed, red-hot annoyance flashing across his face. 'No problem. Now, this is what you'll do—go to that dongoyaro tree near Mr Yaro's house and cut me three strips of cane. Make sure you select well. If you bring me nonsense, I will test it on you first.' He paused to catch his breath. 'Be quick about it,' he added.

I shut the door behind me and, before anything else, crossed the road to check with Agogo-Igbala. He'd not seen Biggie that day. If Biggie wasn't over at Agogo-Igbala's, surely he was at his friend's, Ibrahim's. I took my leave, turned the corner and headed up the estate fleetfooted, my eyes scanning every porch and backyard in the fading daylight. The Lawanis, it appeared, were having a small party or meeting; cars clogged the space in front of their house, and voices swelled from their brightly-lit living room. Old Soldier sat outside with Agaba, the wobbly blue table between them, no snuff or radio on it this time. I wondered if Agaba had flashed Old Soldier his penis too, felt grateful he couldn't flash me now.

Still walking, I noted how unusually quiet it was in the estate. Other than the two men, everyone was indoors, and it had been so all day. I noted, too, how much more tolerable the heat was. Then I remembered it had rained all night, and like every other time after a downpour, people rarely hung outside since the sun did not emerge with its usual venom and the heat did not threaten to suffocate. My legs were tiring. I slowed my pace, wondered what the odds were that someone had seen Biggie.

By the time I reached Ibrahim's house and learned Biggie hadn't been there all that day, I'd run out of places to look for him. I turned around and retraced my steps to the dongoyaro, broke off the *limberest* lowest-hanging switches the circumference of my forefinger, and then I stripped them clean of the leaves and returned home. My parents stared at me for a full minute, their expressions a rictus of shock, when I explained to them no one had seen Biggie that day.

'He'll come back and meet me here,' my mother said finally.

Seven in the evening, and Biggie still hadn't returned. My stomach churned, the borborygmus uncharacteristically persistent. I felt as though I shared in Biggie's infraction. Every time I heard the front door creak open, I rushed out to the living room, but it was just my mother restless, checking to see if Biggie was anywhere in sight, the cane in her hand just as eager. When it was half past eight and Biggie still hadn't returned, my father switched off the TV, left the house quietly and knocked on a few doors to ask the same question we'd all been asking. My mother went after him. This time they forgot all about the canes. The answer was the same; no one had seen Biggie. Before long, a small clutch of neighbours had rallied outside our house, offering ditties and assurances they didn't believe themselves.

'Children of nowadays, that's how they behave. Once they stop letting you bathe them, they think they're grown.'

'The Biggie I know is not like this. He'll come back soon. I'm sure he has a good explanation.'

'Maybe he lost track of time, and now he's scared to come home because he thinks there's punishment waiting for him.'

'Don't overthink it. Children will always be children.'

By nine, everyone had returned home at some point to fetch

their flashlights, so the group was now a small search party. There were at least twenty people, all of them bright-eyed and bushy-tailed, brimming with energy even though it was past some of their bedtimes. Strategies were mapped out, routes assigned, then right as we made to set out, a shrill cry went up in the distance drawing all of our attention. Our eyes shone, our ears perked, and our hearts drummed in our ears.

'What was that?'

'Someone screamed.'

'One of the lookouts, perhaps.'

'Have they found him?'

'It's Biggie, isn't it?'

'He's returned, hasn't he?'

A strange stiffness hijacked the already-tense atmosphere. The air, flimsy and exhale-on-skin warm, seemed to halt. As though our spirits were tethered, we began to move, all of us as one. We hurried in the direction of the voice, curiosity firing up our insides. Everywhere, incandescent white light beamed from flashlights, puncturing the semi-darkness. As we neared the road, whispers fell from every lip.

'Is it him?'

'Did he return?'

'My God.'

'Stop them.'

'Don't let them come any closer.'

'Don't—'

The whispers swelled and became murmuring that spread quickly until some of it reached my father's ears and he hastened his footsteps, even more determined now to see for himself what the ruckus was about. My mother followed behind, her hands on her chest as if holding her heart in place. I struggled to keep up as together we pushed forward through the human traffic. Soon we were in front, staring down at a small cluster of men encircling something. The voices came again.

'Move back.'

'Give room.'

'Space.'

'We need space.'

'No. Stop them.'

'Don't, don't allow . . .'

But it was too late. My parents had already seen it, I'd already seen it—the unmoving form sprawled out on the ground, the tarmac beneath it pooling with something liquid and dark. Something red. Hands gripped my parents by the elbow, attempting to lead them away. My father shrugged himself free. My mother had little say in the matter. She craned her neck, rubbernecking, the cry frozen solid in her throat. Someone pulled me away. But not before a curious beam fell briefly on the figure, across something that looked like a neck sliced half-open, blood misting, the form still.

I felt my breath cease, my fingers go numb. Then I was shivering. My head ached. My eyes stung with unshed tears, and my chest heaved with tidal rhythm. The arm continued to steer me away, back toward my house. That was when my mother let it out, an otherworldly scream, the sound of pain, of grief inconsolable, and I knew then that I'd seen correctly. It was Biggie.

I wasn't present for the rest of it—they wouldn't allow it—but I'd hear later that they followed the trail of blood on the tarmac; the trail led them to Agaba's threshold. Then they barged in to find the house largely empty except for the mattress and plastic table and chairs and one or two squeaky-clean—perhaps even unused— pots and utensils and a kerosene stove. They found blood too in spatters across the walls and thick black clotting puddles on the naked cement floor. A bloodied kitchen knife lay in a corner by the wall; beside it, C-size Tiger batteries and a shattered radio. Hands clasped on his head, Old Soldier explained that Agaba had sold him the mattress earlier that evening. He'd had no idea what the man was up to, but now that he did, it was best they burned it all. When someone asked why a man Agaba's age would have so few belongings, the answer became apparent—it wasn't his first time. A vagrant paedophile who plotted for months until he'd carried out the deed and then moved on.

Later when they'd burned it all and shrouded Biggie with an old akwete wrapper to hide the gash on his neck, when they'd called an ambulance and sat around in our living room to console and wait, Agogo-Igbala hobbled in with reluctance. His eyes were liquid and bloodshot, his nose dribbled with snot. He knelt beside the body and laid a hand on the wrapper, over the moist bloodstained neck region. It lasted only a few minutes, but they could have sworn they saw his hand glow until it was a shimmering neon green. And when he removed it, tears flowing freely from his eyes, it stayed phosphorescent. Without a word, he stood up and left, his steps faltering this time from more than just the limp. Long after he'd gone, their gazes alternated between door and corpse, unsure what to expect. Nothing happened.

And then there was a cough. Then absolute silence. Another cough. More silence. And the corpse lifted its head, or attempted to, causing everyone to gasp and draw back with fright, their legs hanging in the air. The corpse moved again. This time, there was scampering and shrieking from men and women alike. A few people had already made it out the door before my father came forward and uncovered Biggie's face to see him staring back, doe-eyed, confused. When he searched and felt around Biggie's neck, turning him this way and that with frantic motions, the wound was gone, sealed, as though it had never existed.

Then came the loud blaring of siren and flashing red-and-blue lights, and right as the ambulance pulled up outside, another scream erupted. Startled gazes scoured the room meeting other startled gazes, one thought on everyone's mind: 'Was there a second victim?'

'Where did it come from?' someone asked. Another pointed in the direction of Agogo-Igbala's house.

One by one, they filed out, moving like ants to sugar, dreading what they might find. This time there was no kid. They found Agogo-Igbala splayed out in the dust in his backyard, his face ashen, a wound identical to Biggie's gaping from his neck. That was when they understood it all, that with every healing, Agogo-Igbala claimed the infirmity and gave away bits of himself, that Biggie's resurrection had overwhelmed him, that he'd known this would happen hence the tears and reluctance. I wondered if he'd have done it for anyone else, sacrificed himself like that.

Later after much probing, Biggie would reveal to my mother—and my mother only—how he'd gone squirrel hunting outside the estate. How as he returned, Agaba had invited him in, knocked him over the head with something hard, maybe a radio, and stuffed his mouth with a rag before binding his hands and legs. How he'd been only half-conscious, his head heavy and pounding like an anvil, his vision blurred, when a voice like Old Soldier's had come asking about a mattress. How, later, after Agaba was done with the intruder, he'd come back inside, pulled down his trousers and, and . . . How, gagged still, Agaba had loosened the restraints, helped him re-dress and urged him not to disclose the incident. How he'd barely finished nodding before feeling the calloused hand clamp his mouth from behind, then the biting pain in his neck, the warm wetness, the weakness. Perhaps Agaba had changed his mind, done it to give himself a good head start. Or maybe he'd done it before, and this was just his MO. Once the man left, he'd dragged himself up onto wobbly knees and, with the last of his strength, ran.

A month later, on the eve of our departure, my mother would

find the words to narrate these details to me—for my own safety, she'd add—and as she told this last part, she'd sigh, look me straight in the eye and tell me leaving was best for all of us. Then she'd wear a blank stare, nod slowly and say something that, zoned out, I'd completely miss. When I asked what it was, she'd repeat: 'When a child happens upon a hyena and a two-headed goat, which animal calls the most attention?'

SECRET STORIES OF KOYOGELA STREET
Moses Abukutsa

Sofia is an octopus. Streets, like tentacles, stretch from her body and become intersections—some heading to Sofia, Kenya, others to Sofia, Uganda. On Koyogela, one of its frenetic Ugandan streets filled with shops, pubs and brothels, the air reeks of transgression. Two gaunt men stomp into a ditch, huff and rise from the dust onto their wobbly feet, hesitate. One lights a cigarette; the other whistles and blows the cigarette's smoke towards a girl minding her night affairs. Then they walk through my conscience and stagger into Kyambogola Bar.

I rest my conscience and Yamaha motorcycle on a pillar by the bar's entrance and trundle in after the two staggering strangers. The bar is *filled* with the acridness of sweat, the hollering of feisty drunkards and the seductive giggling of girls—some of them waitresses who cruise from table to table, scribbling bills and taking orders and flashing plastic smiles. Mishikaki beef chops and roast chicken hawkers walk in and out. Kenyan rough accents grate against smooth Ugandan courtesies. Customers are mostly Kenyan truck drivers—and a handful of Congolese and Rwandese—in transit to South Sudan, D.R.C, Rwanda, and beyond.

From behind a stuffed counter with metal grills, a self-indulgent smile encounter my roaming eyes. The smile, a practised and nuanced one, sits unsentimentally on the bleached face of a priestess in her sanctuary. She is wearing a luminous green gomesi. I unknot my reciprocal smile from the bind of her smile's spell. Some glances away from her, beside her forest of beers and waragi spirits, I pick out a door leading into an inner yard. There, girls with honey-toned skin, beautiful girls that genuflect before men in supplication, stretch my unquenchable curiosity into the darkness beyond.

Many of the girls displaying themselves under the iridescence of discothèque lights—some with wigs and short tight skirts; others with plain hair or shades of red, pink, blue and green hair braids and multicoloured luminous lipstick—lead men like bulls on leashes to the darkness beyond. Underneath the tables, candles burn to repel mosquitoes. Jose Chameleon's music blasts through speakers from four corners of the bar. Indeed, Kyambogola Bar is a melting pot of happiness, frothing with debauchees throughout the night and vomiting chunks of them, staggering, out into Koyogela Street.

After my second drink, I stroll to the counter. The priestess appraises me. She renews the smile on her face. The two gaunt men who staggered in before me snore on a thinly cushioned sofa. There is this other giant, smoking and following me with his binoculars eyes. The black skin-hugging 'security' t-shirt he wears accentuates his burliness. He heaves a young man to his feet. Confused, the young man groans, unzips his trousers, and pisses on the legs of a table. The security man slaps confusion out of him and throws him out.

'Ssebo, the night is closed.'

Of course, mister giant with binoculars eyes—this I say in my heart. 'Madam?' —this I say out loud.

'Ssebo, we are locking down,' the giant snorts.

The two gaunt men are startled from their snoring. They rise, knock into each other, and stagger out as I cup my nose from the pungency of urine and vomit in the bar.

'Of course, but beer is not closing.' I speak through my fingers. 'I need a room for the night.'

'That will be nine thousand Uganda money, ssebo,' the priestess says.

'Can I find safe parking for my motorcycle?'

'Pay for a room, and Konyi will show you, ssebo.'

'Ssebo come. This is a cold night. Come.' Even this giant is calling me ssebo. This ssebo thing is too much. 'It needs more than a beer and a room, you understand, this night.'

I free my nose. I am quiet. Encouraged by my silence, he continues, 'And I have been given power over they who warm sheets.' This burly security giant is also a pimp. I chuckle.

'I need alone time.'

'Are you serious?'

I nod.

'If a man wants to help himself, who is Konyi to stand in his way? You Kenyans are funny.'

Konyi has stuffed me in his basket of stereotypes of all my countrymen. But there is hardly time to unload that basket. He helps me chain my Yamaha motorcycle to a metallic pillar in the backyard of the bar, close to a corridor lined with rooms for rent. The rooms are named after cities of the world, and the corridor smells of used latex condoms and sex. I see a man and a giggling girl shuttle out of London. Then there is Kampala, Lusaka, Windhoek, New York, and Moscow. Opposite these are Amsterdam, Nairobi, Lagos, *Johannesbag*, Cape Town, and Cairo. Twelve rooms by my furtive count.

When I return to Kyambogola's discothèque lights, the front door is latched, the place smells of strong detergent, and the priestess has opened a beer for herself. She draws a plastic chair for me. There is something inanimate in her eyes, something intangible and subliminal. Something about her makes me think of the poignant story of a prostitute I heard rebels raped in the Sierra Leonean Civil War and abandoned for dead, but had miraculously recovered. And to celebrate her miracle, she lived her life for revenge against men.

'Konyi, there is a free room?'

'Yes. Moscow is free.'

'You think he can sleep in Moscow? Can you sleep in Moscow?'

'I will, but—' I hesitate.

'Ssebo, pour your story into my heart,' she says, slapping her conscience.

'You see. I am. What I am trying to say—'

'Ssebo, you are trying to say that you are running from your government. You killed a woman in Nakuru.'

I am benumbed for a second, probably more than a second. My heart is a mortar pounding by the pestle of her conviction. She frolics in her chair.

I gather my wits. 'Madam, it is the government running after me.'

'But I tell you,' why doesn't she just skip this telling, 'you killed a woman, *banange*!'

I almost fart. I have heard of these prognosticating queers of Ugandan women. Women who read stars and can read your life in your face; women who disappear for months under the sea and Lake Victoria to harness mystical powers; women who have the power of herbs that make men impotent and give love portions to *mpango wa kando* women to take away other women's husbands. But I did not expect to fall into the clutches of one in my escape.

'Don't be uncomfortable, Ssebo.' She chuckles and belches. 'Everyone who walks in here wants to offload their troubles, and they carry them in their eyes and body. I read the soul in their eyes. I read the language in their body. I read their past and know their future. You are in the right hands. Nalongo fixes things.

Things happen to be fixed, Ssebo. I know you want to go in the underground for a while. If you trust me, I will make you vanish. You will be invisible.'

We drink like we are old comrades. She has offered me refuge. She tells me I am her elder dead brother's reincarnation. He died in the resistance. She says he was my height, tall like elephant grass. That he had my round face and my immature bald head. That he kept a goatee like me. The resemblance, she says, is uncanny, even the way I walk and talk. She tells me the brother knocked out a boy who called her big buttocks and tried to fondle her sprouting breasts when they were in junior high school before the National Resistance Movement of 1986. It is evident they had a strong sibling bond—one she confesses was forged when they were children and smoked dry silks of maize under the eaves of banana leaves on their father's farm in Mukono— which was only broken when he joined the resistance and she was forced to run away when government soldiers came, took turns on her and her mother and executed their father. She fishes these skeletons out of the closet for me, a total stranger, in the heat of beer, in the platitudes of her nostalgia that is as cogent as my uxorious desire to listen. We have drunk into the intimate hours after 3 a.m. when she gets tipsy, abandons her chair and gropes for me like a veteran soldier dreamily gropes for old memories of conquest. The discothèque lights are dimmed now, and the counter's green light permeates the darkness around us, diluting it into a translucent sheet. I am tipsier than her, and my body language is plain. I do not protest when she drags me to a room in the opposite direction of Moscow.

In the morning, I tour Nalongo's body with my eyes. It reminds me of peeling paint on the walls of my father's house. Her face is a museum which sits with memories of heavy makeup. She lights a cigarette and sits up on the bed, which creaks like an ungreased rusty wheelbarrow throughout. The smoke from her cigarette spirals in thin snakes into the rafters of the room. It turns me off even more than the stretch marks around her armpits and the veins on her flabby breasts and the layers of skin hanging on her arms like a creased shirt on a hanger. She has a waistline that is even with her torso. Carefully, strapping layer after layer of her garments on, she dresses. She is soon a snake with new skin, a parody of what I have seen on my tour, the kind that is only achieved by dressing, the kind that comes to the mind of a man trying to peel off stifling layers of guilt.

In the days that follow this night, I become many things to Nalongo. She gets me fake Ugandan number plates and employs my Yamaha motorcycle to ferry crates of beer. I am secretly planning to steal her money and hit the road again. If it goes according to plan and I get the keys to the safe behind the counter, I'll be a thief on top of being a runaway murderer. I have run into plainclothes Kenyan police who have frequently crossed from Sofia, Kenya, under false identities with my photograph in their jackets, but they have not been able to identify me. I walk around with Nalongo's talisman in my pocket, which has made me an invisible fugitive in the eyes of Kenyan law enforcers, or so I believe.

But this freedom is shaken when two of Nalongo's Kyambogola night girls are discovered pregnant. One of the pregnancies, I suspect, is mine. And I wear a fortitudinous fugitive's head on my shoulders. Their pregnancies are well advanced—quite peculiar how they successfully concealed their disagreeable situations until now—and since the fathers of their children are not enthusiastic about taking responsibility, the girls pay their matron one hundred thousand Ugandan shillings for abortions.

She gathers her tools for the abortions at nine on a Saturday night. Congolese rhumba music overwhelms the screeching and shouting from brothels and other overnight bars outside Kyambogola. Her tools rattle in my conscience. Rusty corrugated iron sheet roofs stretch out like dusty blankets under a full moon. At half past ten, I am loitering outside the room where Nalongo is performing her second abortion—on the girl I suspect has my pregnancy. The first job has gone well. Three of the pregnant girls' friends are around.

This is what I have brought to myself: shame. Did I mean to kill? No. It was the trap. I was trapped in one of the Somalia PTSD nightmares. I grabbed her from the bed and threw her onto the tiled floor of our Nakuru apartment, thinking I was in the thick of an ambush. I stepped on her neck. She kicked and moaned, but an alien beast growled in me and stood its ground. I was in Somalia, so I thought at the time, Afmadow to be precise, and in my head I was neutralizing an Al Shabaab terrorist with a Kalashnikov, determined that he should fall under my army counterterrorism training. As I recall events in tonight's conscience, the apartment must by now have been cordoned off from all access, and the military intelligence police must have been turning stones in search of a man, a veteran of Operation 84 in Afmadow and Kismaayo Somalia, a veteran of war in his early thirties with a goatee and a bald head, who is no longer himself. I killed an innocent woman. I murdered my wife: the voice from curtains of darkness returns to haunt me. I am now pacing up and down, pocketing, un-pocketing, counting the stars near the Southern Cross, then the Orion and feeling a cold sweat trickle down my brow. It wasn't my fault, was it? It was the fault of my head that I lost in Somalia. The head which now wanted antidepressant pills, one full of shootings, kabooms and beheadings, an alien head which swings like a pendulum between conscience and PTSD.

'Pa—nya—ko!'

Nalongo wrenches me from conscience. I hesitate. Then I enter the room.

'They are twins refusing to come out. Give me a hand. They want to kill their mother. Sometimes, those with a strong spirit fight back and refuse to come out.'

I think Nalongo has botched this. Her claws tap me into the sight of the girl's bloody thighs.

'Grip her legs.'

She sinks her claws deeper into the girl's spread legs. The girl groans between her teeth. I bite my lip. She screams. I have a bad taste in my mouth. I spit blood in the smell of antiseptic. I badly want a handkerchief. The electricity goes out. One of the friends lights candles. There is the panting and laboured breathing of death in the room.

For three hours, there is a struggle. Everyone around the girl is sweating; candles burn out, and new ones are lit. Nalongo slumps into a plastic chair. She smells of antiseptic, blood, sweat, cigarettes and camphor. She calls for a cigarette and beer. I know it is over. I let go of the girl's legs. They have turned heavy and cold in my hands. The two foetuses are swaddled in layers of bloody dripping sheets. The electricity comes back.

'It is over.'

Nalongo puffs and drinks. The girl's friends, who have followed the whole process in anxious silence, convene like a multicoloured wreath of heads around the bed. They exchange knowing looks. One rips off her red wig and breaks from the wreath. Another screams.

'No screaming, Rita. No screaming. I want Konyi.' Nalongo puffs.

Konyi storms in, the scar on his upper lip more prominent than ever. He rubs his eyes and buttons up his shirt. He locks the door behind him. A candle's flame expires in the wind the shutting door sweeps in. He scrutinizes particular faces in the room—the dead body, me, Nalongo.

'You do what you do. Umna Kenya will help you.'

Nalongo's luminous green gomesi flaps in apparitions of thick, flowing cigarette smoke as she strolls out. The beer bottle, empty like her soul, swings in her hand. And in muffled sobs, the girls' friends scatter their wreaths into the empty night she leaves behind.

I have become something unknown. I am piqued. Death, I have seen before. But death so casual like the present one melts even the steel out of the most unconscionable of soldiers. Yes, I am here because I murdered and I am running from the law, trying to find peace. But I did not want to kill. It was the absence of antidepressant pills. I hate dead bodies. Death should not be handled this casually, especially where life is supposed to be given. Death has to achieve a goal, a higher purpose, like the extermination of evil or the peace of a nation. But this sogginess in dripping sheets, the death of our future, is for Nalongo's absurd comedy and my ephemeral relief. Even dogs have died better deaths.

Konyi lights something I have never smoked. He scraped it from the pockets of his trousers. After puffing it three times, he passes it over. For what I have become, I have no moral authority to decline; it is after all the only escape anyone can presently get. Three puffs defrost the pique in my body. Konyi walks out, returns with a sack, fits it over the girl's naked body, and binds it with a nylon string.

I pick the three soggy foetuses, now stuffed in black polythene, and plod after him with the sack on his shoulders. We take the back entrance of Kyambogola, away from Sofia's Koyogela Street. A cloud eclipses the full-beyond-midnight moon. The dark shadow of the cloud swallows our plodding. Konyi walks like a man going to incinerate plastic bottles and dump broken beer bottles in a dustbin. He has probably done this before. With a frequency only his silence knows. Konyi must be fickle and cold-blooded. If Ugandan police chance upon us, he will probably not hesitate to sell me out. A gust of wind whistles over my face taking these thoughts with it. I sigh. We jump over a broken sewerage pipe. Konyi spits, forgetting that he has a lit cigarette between his lips. It tumbles into the broken sewerage pipe, and its glow dies in a hiss. When we have crossed several blocks of mud houses and shacks, panting and sweating, he stops at the shell of a rusty pickup before a dumpsite hillock. Motioning me to the hillock, he dumps the girl's limp body on the back of the pickup shell and stands beside it like it's an unforgotten memory from war.

'Umna Kenya, we are undertakers. We are movers and shakers.'

I hope his mind has not left him as he wipes his hands on his trousers. The insanity we have just carried is of the kind that eats away at a man's soul.

'Not by choice,' I whisper, and discard the foetuses.

'Umna Kenya, Nalongo is the power. She is the priestess of Koyogela Street. We worship in Kyambogola Bar, her shrine.' He lights a cigarette. 'She told me you murdered a woman, is it true?'

'So what if it is true?' I am slightly irritated. 'Then it is true you know everything she knows.'

'She is a pig in a pigsty, and I am mud.' He puffs out. 'Can a pig in a pigsty live without mud?' Something stirs. Two dogs are fighting over the foetuses. I shake the stone that is the head on my shoulders.

'A pig in a pigsty.'

'Correct.'

'Sofia, Koyogela Street, Kyambogola are pigsties.'

'Correct.'

'The world is a pigsty.'

'Ssebo, that is why you murdered?'

'Maybe.'

'And she was your wife?'

I sharply turn my gaze from the dogs; they have divided spoils. My hands tremble, my feet grow weak, and my knees almost fold. Sweat trickles down my armpits. Before Konyi, I am a vile human being.

'Don't look surprised. There are no secrets in that woman's breast that I haven't sucked.'

I can tell Konyi has slept with Nalongo probably more than I can guess, and he thinks of me as a liability he should get rid of—and is trying to figure out how and when to do it. I do not intend to let him have that pleasure.

'She took you to Luwemba for rites.'

'You know that too?' The words stagger out of my throat, floating in the stream of his cigarette smoke.

'She invites you to her room three nights every week. Last time was Wednesday. And you have meticulously guarded the secret of this dead girl's affair from her. You are a man.'

'Man to man, have I crossed a line?'

Konyi laughs. 'There is a cunning old she owl, a mistress of the night who steals souls. She whispers. She claws. She sucks blood. She kills. But don't you worry, honey shall flow. You will be preserved, probably. Keep memories. Hang only on every pleasure of their wisdom. There is poison in cunning old blankets and parables from old women's beds. A man like you who went to school should not find his soul plundered.'

'So these are the happy days of men.'

'Imagine the days of sorrow to come.' He shrugs and discards the butt of his cigarette. 'Men, we are trees. We blossom sorrows that take away strength from here and here.' He slaps his chest and points his head. 'Sometimes happiness flowers into memories, but when memories of happiness fail to produce fruits of love, there is famine. We become barren trees of bitterness and death.'

We trundle back to Kyambogola, Konyi's rushing river of words guiding us. If Nalongo told him that I killed Samba, then she trusts him and he knows her. But can there be trust in a world where there is no conscience? This tentacle of an octopus that is Sofia's Koyogela Street could easily constrict me into the life sentence awaiting me on the other side. I should hasten my plan to steal and run soon, maybe to northern Uganda, perhaps Gulu, or even cross into South

Sudan, hitchhiking on a truck. I could even make a fortune trading in precious metals in DRC. I know Nalongo will only keep me up to the point she no longer feels I entertain her nights. Then, like thunder, she will strike and execute her revenge.

'Why did you murder your wife?' Konyi asks, cutting through my thoughts.

'PTSD. I skipped my antidepressants.'

'PTSD— there is no PTSD, only actions of weak minds or strong minds. Or cover-ups that have no clothes and need underwear.' The way he speaks with authority about everything, like he is not just here for his muscles. 'Good night, ssebo. Don't skip your antidepressants.' I hear the snigger in his voice.

'Good night.'

Darkness swallows me. I fall deeply into sleep the moment I slip under the blanket. Noise in the street of pubs and brothels rouses me up in the late hours of Sunday morning. The octopus tentacle that is Koyogela Street seemingly has drawn out its suckers in the form of a rowdy throng. Restlessness stalks the dust raised from their feet, scampering toward a musty dreadlocked madman, pulling the pickup with a rope. This is synergy. I am stunned. I join the throng. They have kept their distance at the front of Kyambogola. My eyes catch the body. It is hers. The sack that was her coffin is missing. Her clothes have been stripped from her. It now hits me how stupid it was for Konyi to dump a girl's body on an open pickup shell near a dumpsite. But whether it was stupid or strategic, the body is now here, mutilated and tied with a sisal rope. Her left breast is gone, her open mouth is a cave of darkness, her right leg is amputated from the ankle, and her eyes are empty sockets of grief. Her organs have been harvested. The madman laughs maniacally. He waves off flies with his dreadlocks that stretch out like snakes from his head.

'He is taking her to Luwemba.'

'The police must come.'

'Uganda Police, so, to do what?'

'Measure fingerprints.'

'But she has no fingers.'

The last statement from Nicodemus, a night watchman who guards the beer depot, the Kinyozi with unsterilized machines where men cut their hair, and a hairdressing shop across Kyambogola bar, makes my stomach boil. A dust devil blows a wedge-like path through the people closest to the pickup and the madman, scattering papers into the turmoil of voices. Konyi joins me. Nalongo and all the girls, including those who were with us last night, join the throng.

'Ssebo. Run.'

Before Konyi's words crystalize in my ears, Nalongo screams. She throws herself on the pickup, weeping and waving her hands in the air. She wears a sparkling yellow gomesi dress. The girls watch her sobbing hysterically. She throws dust into her hair and pulls at it. She bangs at the rusty metal of the pickup. A woman takes a leso from her waist and covers the body. Then Luwemba arrives. And the throng, as though sliced with a sharp knife, parts for him. Even the madman stops pulling and steps aside. Nalongo kneels before one of the pickup's headlamp holes and rolls on the ground, a groaning mass of grief. I am beginning to tire of her melodrama when silence falls on everyone like the sudden cease of a massive rainfall. Luwemba speaks.

'He is around. The killer is here. The one who killed this girl killed his wife. He is a stranger from Kenya. His name is Panyako.'

The words shackle my legs. There is a cunning old owl. Konyi's words tumble over each other in my head. They unshackle my legs. Run. Fight. Or. Be killed. My head swirls. It is hot. I see things. I see people coming for me. It feels like I am trapped again, triggered. This is another ambush. But where is my Kalashnikov? This must be the end.

*

We left the camp at Afmadow yesterday evening and have been leading our convoy towards Kismaayo. At 11 a.m., after our commander says it is 15 Kilometres of Acacia and Savannah bush to Kismaayo, a landmine goes off. There are gunshots behind us. On my left flank, my comrade's head is blown off, and his torso crumbles on his limbs. My heart races; it is an overheating kettle of steaming water. So I am going to die in Somalia. The image of my daughter, the last I saw of her in her school uniform, flashes across my face. The weight of my gun and the heavier weight of my apprehension stir me into bloodthirstiness. Shouts of 'death to all kafirs' whirl; machine guns growl. I return fire for fire. Two more comrades are neutralized beside me. Grenades thunder. Rockets fly over my head. I crouch after ducking past a truck forced to surrender with deflated tyres. Ten trucks form an impregnable wall for our regrouping. I fire incessant shots which decapitate several heads, maybe five, maybe more, I don't care. They are trophies. I have taken cover behind a tank, on top of several dead men, not less than six. Several trucks have flattened tyres, and the sun shoots needles of beams through the bullet holes in one of the trucks, forming dapples of light on the tawny grass in its shade.

This is the pit of malfeasance. But no, the end cannot be near; I am enveloped by darkness. When I come to consciousness, something like rain falls on my face. Someone has poured a jug of water over me. My body is wet. Hands grip me. They pull me into a truck. Shots are still ringing. Foreign accents clatter in my ears. Where am I? It is not Somalia. It is not Afmadow. It is not Kismaayo. My eyes are stinging with grime. I cannot see ahead.

Finally, the hands dump me on a hard floor. My head spins, and I swear I can see the floor moving. Someone says, 'He has lost a lot of blood.' But I do not remember being shot. I only remember a man, Konyi, telling me to run. I cannot remember any pain penetrating my body. I only remember the blackout. A bright light flashes across my face, the sun. And my eyes open in narrow slits. I am lying on my back in a van. Something hard and broken presses my thigh. It is the talisman in my pocket. Curious faces in Uganda Police uniforms wielding guns surround me. I can hear people shout obscenities in Luganda. I can hear women weeping and girls cursing my name.

'Panyako ni makwerekwere.' I hear Nalongo's unmistakable soprano above all voices, spouting the word South African jingoists call 'foreigners' during xenophobic riots. The van jolts. The throng running behind it pelts any rotten thing their hands can get, and the rotten things plop into my conscience. I turn my head away and spit out blood; tears sting the grime in my eyes—I know I am going away and will never return to the secret life.

THE ANATOMY OF FLYING THINGS
Enit'ayanfe Ayosojumi Akinsanya

Abami peeped through the crack in the mountains to gauge the sorrow in her lover's eyes. What startled her was not what she saw but what she did not see. She saw the sorrow but not her lover's face. A peek into the future. The provenience of her dream. A road rolling out like a tongue, stretching into the human world, wending in-between thickets that stabbed the sepia-purple air like the antlers of a stag. She stole through the offshoots, teased the earth with her soles, and disappeared into the mist.

Behind her, her one and true love ululated into the void as though he were the one lost.

She found her first human at the mouth of a forest. He was squatting behind a shrub of strange plants, his funny-looking body-secrets unwrapped to his thighs. A smell she had never smelled before struck her nose like a direct affront, and no, it did not come from the stump in his hand that trailed a thin smoke. It came from his behind, the curved shadow between his lowered body-secrets and the skin of his upper body, from where brown lumps spooled downward.

'What are you staring at? You never see pesin wey dey shit before?'

he barked at her, his gruff voice cutting through her heart. But when he took her hand afterwards and led her out of the jungle, his palm was gentle. He smelled differently, as though what happened behind the shrub was an imagined past. He asked her why she was dressed funny, wads of raffia clinging to her breasts, a raffia tutu at her waist, her feet shoeless, henna-like marks on her face like tattoos. He asked her if she was part of a theatre group since the city crawled with crowds like that. She shook her head, half-confused. He asked her if she was Igbo because he was from the East. She shook her head in more confusion. He asked her what her name was. She told him, amused by her own quickness to return his language. In her childhood, when she flew beneath the hood of Isalu, with her sister and friends, sitting in their cockpit of strung-together calabash pieces, the wind sometimes blew snatches of human talk into their ears, and they would play little word games with what they had heard. Those moments had always glittered with astral luminescence, an epiphany about a world so different, so unknowable, that it suddenly became what *must* be known. She knew she had to leave Isalu someday. It had been a game; now she was living the game.

'You talk funny,' he told her when they reached the streets where travel portals that looked like horses without manes zipped up and down, carrying people past ginormous contraptions that in turn roared and rumbled, blazing harsh light from holes that looked like giant eyes. She should be terrified. Her sister *would* be terrified. Her friends, too. But after the first sliver of a shiver that ran through her, she buzzed with the expectation of a mad adventure.

He laughed. 'You look like a child. Your eyes wey dey shine like that.' His fingers tightened around her wrist. 'Come. Before we part, let us go to one place.'

And they vanished behind a rank of unlit houses into the city's shadows.

Morning streaked all over his face, like the strobe light of Isalu when the elders wanted to know which girl was unspoiled and which was already spoiled. She felt the irony settle in her stomach like a rock. It was her first time, and it had excited her when he touched her. They had not behaved like strangers, and they had overslept. From what she and her friends had gathered during their childhood flights, humans saw blood when it was their first time. Maybe that was why he had continued thrusting and still had the peace to sleep till now, because there had been no blood with her. No pain, either. Just an opening inside her like a new beginning. She wondered now what he had thought while brushing aside the raffia between her legs. When he had reached up to her chest to remove her raffia bowls, she had held his roaming hands and whispered, 'body-secrets,' which made him chuckle and left her strangely embarrassed. It had startled her that her body-secrets had not startled him out of his desire. The men of the human world, of this city, did not seem to care about what you had on your body before they climbed you.

She had woken up first; the softness and strangeness of the bed unsettled her. She rocked him awake like a baby. Kohl rimmed his eyes as though he had lined them that morning. He hadn't. It was one of the reasons she had wanted to leave Isalu: the beauty of the human body. The males of Isalu had different bodies, bodies that floated, nebulous bodies. Now that her dream had solidified, she could no longer think of them as men, as *male*. This man—this man who lay with her and married her body to her dream—*he* was her pinnacle. He opened his eyes. He peered at her for a while as though he needed an explanation from her. Then he said, 'Oh,' and leaned on one arm, his shoulder rubbing against his jaw. He passed his hand down his face. He looked different from a baby now, with red in his eyes and his nose rumpled. He turned to pull out the drawer by the bed, from where he had taken the rubber thing he had slipped on himself the previous night before sliding into her.

'Where we come?' she asked.

He jerked around, intrigued. 'That's the second full sentence you've said since we met.'

There was something about the way he said it, 'since we met', that sounded like the sealing of a fate. He stopped talking, his head bent, as though he needed to find the right word to tell her.

'We came to a place where we could have fun undisturbed,' he said. 'People like us that are not together and who cannot take each other home come here all the time. Before they say goodbye to each other.'

'Ah,' she said and fell silent.

'Who are your people? Where are they?' he asked, and she flinched as if he had waved a knife in her face. Her sister would be disappointed. Her friends would be frightened for her. Her mother would, of course, be distraught. Her father would not be; he had always called her wayward. And then there was her lover, Kayefi, whose doleful eyes had been unable to stop her from flying.

He rolled something between his lips, wetting the length with his tongue. He fetched what looked like a flame-maker from the drawer and held it to the tip of the paper-like thing. Then he paused and left it on the drawer, unlit.

'You are one of those girls, aren't you?'

She waited for him to continue, so she could make sense of his words. Perhaps he should have asked if she ran from home; she would have nodded. But he sighed instead. He heaved himself off the bed and went to stand by the window. His behind had left a groove on the foam; she stared down at it, charmed by the perfect contours. She gazed up at his body, the clefts and the ridges, the long, dangling cocoon between his ripped legs. It had made her cry softly and gratefully through the night, pushing all the way into her stomach and causing her knees to buckle and weaken.

'Your name,' she said. 'You not tell me. But I tell you my name.'

He smiled. His lips had taken on an angle she could not really name. They looked rather sad.

'My name is Egbo.'

She tasted the word like food, her first meal in the human world.

'You must be hungry,' he said, surprising her. Did humans read minds? She and her people at Isalu had never been able to. He startled her again. 'Can I change your name?'

She let out a long shrill sound. It was supposed to be laughter. Then she nodded.

He took her home. She smiled at the way he walked close to her, holding her hand and sauntering into the compound as though she were a prize he had won from a conquest. There was a man in the compound wearing severe-looking body-secrets and small glass windows over his eyes—and bending over on a bench to pull what looked like small underwear over his feet. Egbo introduced him as Teacher Ayo. 'He teaches mathematics, but he does not understand it.'

Teacher Ayo sneered back at him, 'You have brought home another theatre arts freak, you this unserious man.'

'They give the best sex,' Egbo retorted, then looked hurt as though he had unexpectedly bitten his own tongue.

Teacher Ayo carried his flat bag and strode out, yelling, '*Okada! Okada!*' until one of those zipping up-and-down objects—that looked like Isalu's royal horses—stopped beside him, and he climbed on it and was zipped away. A man wearing a long, white body-secret and holding a big book stood by the wall, peeing. Was this how humans behaved, doing private things in the presence of others, not minding who saw them? As he entered the compound and saw them, he clutched the big book to his chest, shut his eyes, and started vibrating. Her language dribbled out of his mouth, a fluent outpouring, and she gasped. How did this human know the language of her people? Later, when she learnt new human words, she would be surprised—and a little offended—to hear the people of the compound call it 'gibberish'. As she tried to touch the man, she was mystified to see him brandish the big book at her like a weapon and to hear him say, now in human tongue, 'Spirit of the other world. Unclean spirit. I bind you, I cast you.'

'Oh, shut up, Pastor,' Egbo said. 'You no go revival today?'

Pastor ran into the house, still waving the big book. A boy darted out of the house, his upper body-secrets tucked into his lower body-secrets like those of Teacher Ayo. A short woman scampered behind him, holding a strange-looking flask in a strange-looking basket, screaming, 'Stop, Bode, or I will spank you.'

The boy giggled as if it were a joke. 'Star Boy,' he screamed as he raced past. 'Hey, Bod-Bod, my guy!' Egbo responded, and they hit their palms together. Abami did not know what Bode was supposed to be, but he looked like a tiny teacher.

'This angry woman, don't touch that boy o,' Egbo called after the running woman. She raised her middle finger at him and disappeared after the boy behind the outer wall.

Abami watched Egbo laugh for a while. 'Why call you Star Boy?' she asked.

He told her he was a music artiste, a local champion for street festivals, and that he sang like Wizkid. She did not understand half of what he said, but the way he said it, his shoulders raised, a self-satisfied grin on his face, made it sound like it was meant to be important. A star boy shitting in the bush. She wanted to laugh, but he was already showing her to a woman who sold brown fluids in bottles that looked unwashed. The woman turned to look at them. She called him Star Boy too and smiled and raised her thumb at him, patting the body of the bottle with her other hand.

'Nne Nsogbu,' he said to her, 'I go need am, but not now.'

Nne Nsogbu looked like trouble, but she had a happy face. The woman stretched out her hand. Was this how humans greeted? Back at Isalu, you gripped the person by the waist and tumbled them to the ground and stuffed their mouth with sand.

He pulled her into his room and showed her his guitar. 'This place is called Ojuelegba.' Piles of books were on his table as though he were a student. They looked like they had not been opened for ages. Students in Isalu had books too, but they found it easier to listen to the books than to open them. Maybe that was what he did, too—listen. His table was the biggest thing in this place which would not pass for a cubicle in Isalu. He watched her inspect his room like a scene.

'This is where I live. I study sociology at the state university. Schools are on strike now, and I wanted to travel back to the East. But now that we've met—' He flicked a spider from the wall. He looked up at her, and because of his eyes, she remembered the night before. 'It just feels wrong to leave you alone in this big, crazy city.'

He told her about kidnapping, about girls that entered beautiful cars and were driven away and never seen again, at least not in their full bodies. He told her about unexpected gunshots, people fighting randomly on the streets and breaking things and injuring people sitting outside their homes, things that he must have expected to scare her—because when she sat on his mattress and tapped her legs on the carpet excitedly, he looked scared. He obviously didn't understand that she didn't understand, couldn't understand, just yet.

He didn't look scared, though, when she vomited the first food he gave her. He called it 'fried rice' and grumbled for hours that he had bought it with good money, and she just wasted it like that.

'Why you not ever cook?' she asked him in defence, as though what he cooked could not possibly nauseate her and his laziness was the reason for her sickness. There were pots and pans in his room that she was sure he had never used.

He laughed like she did not know what she was talking about. But she turned her back and would not speak to him until he said, 'Okay, okay. You win. We will go to the market.' He paused. 'But first, we gats change your look o. You can't follow me to the market like this. People will not sell to us.'

It was a tug of war. She accused him of wanting to steal her body-secrets. He replied, 'Girl, we slept together. You removed my *own* body-secrets.' She finally let him hand her a long dress that felt like a thin stream running over her body. It left her arms bare and scared her. He laughed. 'Don't worry, you won't boil to death. It's better than the raffia and leaves. You are not a masquerade.'

They went to the market and bought tomatoes and peppers and rice, which she wanted to eat straight from the huge bags propped by the stalls. He had to restrain her. He bought her a pair of high-heeled shoes. But when they got home and she tried them on, she collapsed on his bed, and he worried that she had sprained her ankles. But she was laughing, and so he started to laugh too.

On the stove, rice boiled.

The first time she ate a cockroach in his presence, he stopped touching her. They were in bed, and he was tickling her, and she was squirming and shrieking when something flew across the room, a buzzing brown blur, and she aimed for it with the expertise of a hunter. She held its antenna and held it above her face. The insect wriggled until she dropped it in her mouth, despite him shouting, 'No, no, no,' beside her. He scrambled from the bed and ran outside. She ran after him, and they both ran back inside.

'You are lucky there are people outside, and I just don't want to disgrace myself before them,' he said, panting, wagging a finger at her. 'How would it sound? "The girl going out with Star Boy eats cockroaches." How can *anybody* eat cockroaches?'

He said it as if he expected her to laugh, but it was the first time she felt he was ashamed of her.

The day after the cockroach incident, somebody came to bang on their door. He opened it, and a young woman flew in. She wore only one earring, a hoop like a car's tyre. She made straight for the mattress, where Abami sat trying to read mathematics from one of Egbo's secondary school textbooks, and then she stopped short, ran her painted eyes up and down Abami, and started to clap and screech.

'Eh-eh-ehhh! Wonders shall never end!' She whirled around to face Egbo. 'Egbo, na this kind girl you carry go market? This dirty girl looking at a maths textbook like say na novel she dey read? Do you know that people saw you? How dare you embarrass me like this!' She spun back around to glare at Abami.

'Chioma, what are you doing here?' Behind her, Egbo sounded like a cornered animal.

The woman's eyes bulged. 'What am I doing in my boyfriend's room?'

'We broke . . . never mind. You, you were not supposed to show up until next month. Are you not doing your IT in Sagamu again?'

The young woman, Chioma, pounced on him and started pummelling his chest, shouting, 'You cheat, you bastard! I have nothing more to say to you. My brother will hear about this.' She snapped her fingers and flew out of the room.

Silence fell. Abami clutched her chest and backed away from Egbo as he reached out to touch her.

He did not tell her why he hid his relationship from her and what he now planned to do, and she stopped asking after many hours. That same afternoon, when school children came back, she went out into the compound to sit with the boy, Bode.

'Let's make a deal, Aunty Abami. I will teach you to speak English while you teach me maths.'

She rubbed his head. She felt like crying. The word 'maths' fanned alive in her mind an image of Egbo, an image she didn't want right then. 'But me not know maths. Me not know maths at all.'

Bode pursed his lips. 'Do adults lie? I have seen you with Brother Egbo's textbook many times o.'

'Bode, don't stress that woman,' Nne Nsogbu called from her kiosk, where she was wiping a bottle with a piece of cloth. 'Where is your mother sef?'

'She has gone to a burial party,' Bode answered.

'And left you locked outside with your school bag and no food. These city women *sha*.'

She plucked a Gala sausage from her kiosk and threw it at the boy, who caught it with a grin. He pointed it in Abami's direction, but Abami shook her head.

'Maybe she wants one too,' Nne Nsogbu said, yanking out another Gala and aiming it at Abami. But Abami raised her hands and shook her head vigorously. Her stomach was a storm, and she would certainly throw up. Nne Nsogbu shrugged and stuck the Gala in her own mouth.

Abami rose and walked back into the house. She found Egbo standing in nothing but briefs, his towel draped across his neck. He told her he was going to a show.

'I want come,' she said.

'No!'

She stepped back. He had raised his voice at her. He softened his voice. 'No, you can't.'

'You, avoid me outside.'

'What?'

'You, very ashamed of me.'

He shook his head as if to say that she had misjudged him, picked up a pail and went out to the bathroom.

When he returned the following morning, he stank of beer, and she did not let him touch her because this was a new smell.

'You say my name, you change it. You not change it.'

'Huh?'

He had started forgetting things about her. He was also keeping late nights. And strange men often came looking for him in the compound, promising to kill him if they caught him. The day she glimpsed them attacking him by the end of the street, he ran up the road into the house and bolted the door of the room and asked her not to open the door for anyone unless he told her to. But nobody came to the door, and he passed out on the bed, exhaustion over his face like a pall.

That same evening, after he woke up, he brushed his teeth, splashed water on his face, wore a shirt she had never seen on him before, carried his guitar, and left the house.

He did not return home until three days after. And when he returned, the first thing he did was yell at Bode, who was telling Abami he got nine marks out of ten in maths, just as Egbo was walking into the compound.

'You never do that,' she said to Egbo, following him into their room.

'What the fuck are you saying to me?'

'You never shout at Bode before. You shout now.'

'He was calling you a name I don't like.'

'Is my name.'

'So? Was he respecting you?'

'Bode cry.'

He said nothing. He walked out again and, this time stayed out for an entire week. When he returned, he melted into her arms, crying, and finally told her what was going on. He did not want to be with Chioma. He had broken up with her the previous year. He was only stuck with her because her brother, who was the Capone of the cultists on campus, had once loaned him some money for a studio recording session, and he had been unable to pay it back. Chioma was about to aggravate the issue now because she felt slighted by Abami. And she would turn Egbo's greatest fear into a weapon. She had vowed to tell her brother how Egbo broke her heart if he did not pay back the money he owed her brother. Egbo was not sure he wanted to know whether she was bluffing or not. The Capone did not joke with his kid sister and anything to do with her, so Egbo knew he was sitting on a keg of gunpowder. He had been running around these past weeks, showing up at shows he wasn't invited to, begging for a live performance, to raise money. But nothing was working.

'Money plenty?' Abami asked.

He looked puzzled for a while, then, sniffing back in his snot, said, 'Yes, yes. It's a lot of money.'

Abami held him and wished she could cry along with him.

Abami sat in the compound, watching as Pastor trembled and danced by the wall.

'How you know the language of me people?' she asked suddenly.

Pastor dilated his eyes. 'You are a crazy woman. Get thee behind me, Jezebel! *Ribosantasanta.*' He fled behind the wall.

Nne Nsogbu and Bode started laughing. 'Is this one a man of God? This one? Look at his dirty soutane,' Nne Nsogbu said.

Bode doubled up on the bench. His mother had locked him out again. It was dusk, and Teacher Ayo was listening to Cool FM on his radio, avoiding Bode's plaintive stare. Bode had held his homework book open when Teacher Ayo came outside to sit. He wished Teacher Ayo would at least whisper a correct answer. Abami watched their antics quietly. The light of the day drained from the sky. The compound was filling fast with men who needed an evening shot of what Nne Nsogbu sold in brown plastic bottles. They were the same men who clustered at Aboki Newspaper's table in the morning, talking about governors who ate their state's money and ignored the bad roads and floods or arguing about which football team had the best players in history. Tonight, they talked about how the night watch people had found the body of a girl *on the street* and how they were sure it was the work of Yahoo boys who used the bodies of women for money-making rituals. Abami found it both repulsive and fascinating an idea that a woman's body yielded that much. Would her body make money, too? Could she make Egbo rich enough to return Chioma's brother's money? Listening to them all, she felt the sensation of being robbed. It was like while she flew with her people over the dome of the human world and peeked down to admire and to wonder, she had expected to fly down and caress a beautiful painting. But now that she was down, it was not the beauty she had expected; it did not even look like a painting, more like ruins, jagged ruins, because all she could see was a torn canvas.

'Chioma's brother will kill me,' Egbo mumbled into her shoulder later that night. 'They have killed someone before. In my presence. They shot him on campus, and nothing happened to them.'

'You, my anchor here in your world,' she said, patting his back. 'Only you understand me. Where I will go if you leave me?'

That night, she finally cried. That night, they cried together. That night, he slipped into her without sheathing himself with rubber, for the first time.

And, that same night, in the hood close to the sky, an alien baby bled to life.

*

They thought nobody in the compound knew, even though her vomiting became more consistent. But the city's eyes, like its ears, were too alive. They would never have imagined that the story carriers would find Chioma and update her. Egbo swore that he did not tell any soul apart from those at the hospital. Yet, Chioma visited again, this time with some of her brother's men. Men who oozed evil from their pores. They slammed Egbo into the wall and slashed his cheek with small knives. Blood dribbled. Before they left, Chioma sniggered at him. 'This is just a teaser. The movie will begin properly if you don't remove that bastard in her stomach before the end of this week.' She leaned in, close enough for Abami to smell her perfume from where he stood shaking. 'And you dare not disappear. She too. Egbo, my brother doesn't make empty threats. You know.'

He knew. He knew the game of power, how reckless, how irrational it was, how the powerful would insist on making the powerless suffer for daring to put themselves first. It massaged an empty need, and Chioma was determined to have hers assuaged.

Egbo and Abami stepped out of the taxi and gazed at the backdoor clinic's door, their hearts thumping. It was Saturday. The week was ending already. It had been another tussle between them, but this time, Egbo's resolve was slack with fear. Abami barely did much to convince him it might not be the right thing to do, but it was expedient.

'You have been my friend, Egbo, long before you became Star Boy,' the doctor at the clinic had said when Egbo ran to him days before. Let's do this first. We will talk about the bills later. Chioma's people are dangerous. And you owe them. If she says this is what must happen, then it must happen.'

What they did not know—even Abami herself—was that her

body was not fashioned for the human procedure. She was a flyer, a body borne on winds. A body light. A body fragile. The smallest cut would undo her. The human world would undo her. The doctor, with all his education, did not know this. How could he? Even Egbo did not know the woman he had fallen in love with.

So they made her lie behind a screen. So, they cut her, sank sharp things into her body. So, they removed the foetus. So she started bleeding. For hours, she was still a red body brimming forth. The doctor, tired of changing her gowns, petrified of having a case die on his watch, pleaded with Egbo to take her home. Egbo said he would not. What would he tell them when he reached the compound with a bleeding Abami in his arms? What would he tell Nne Nsogbu? Bode—what would he tell the little boy?

They stood beyond the bed, hiding Abami from view with the blue screen, and listened to her grunt and groan and yell and writhe, the bed metal squeaking against the tiles, until there was an engulfing stillness in the room.

He traipsed into the compound like in a trance. The doctor's vociferations about how he could not possibly abandon the body and just leave still echoed in his head. He hardly saw the boy until he almost trod on him on the bench.

'Star Boy, where is Aunty Abami? We were to finish our English lesson this morning. I wanted to teach her words and antonyms. But I didn't see her.'

'I have told you to stop calling her Abami,' he whispered before the shame in his chest bloated outward and ballooned all over his skin.

Nne Nsogbu was there by her kiosk, her accounts book open in front of her, pencil in her mouth like a cigarette.

'Star Boy,' she said, leaning forward. 'Why you dey sweat like this? Wey your girlfriend?'

Egbo stood there, staring up. He could hear the sky wailing; one of the governor's helicopters was plying the clouds. Abami would have held his hand and asked, pointing, 'What that? It fly like me and my people.' And he would have laughed and gently rebuked her for reading his sci-fi novels. She would have made him forget the imbalances of his world. He sat on Nne Nsogbu's bench, beside Bode—in whose small eyes the beginning of a future knowledge was spreading—and started to weep.

ONCE BOYS AND GIRLS OF THE STREAM
Charlie Muhumuza

In those seasons, we woke before the sun could shake off the veil of mist hanging over its face like a bride shyly stepping out of her father's house. Previously, we had waited until we felt the sun's fingers touch our eyelids. If we turned left and still felt its touch, then we woke, our mothers' voices already beckoning. But the older we grew, the earlier we woke, sleeping on our right sides so as to catch sight of the bride through the window, for we had learnt of its wonders. Wonders soon to thin into nothingness.

We would get our yellow plastic jerrycans, whose sizes grew bigger as we grew taller, and head for the stream. When we got to the stream, we tightened the red tops of our jerrycans, removed our shirts, and rolled tight the waistlines of our shorts. Trembling in the morning cold, we breathed in deep, held our breaths and jerrycans and jumped into the freezing stream. Our bodies would shudder awake under the water, and with our chins quivering in the cold, we giggled and made lewd jokes.

When the girls arrived, they would make fun of us for floating on jerrycans, saying we couldn't really swim. So we learnt to swim. First, we tumbled, then we kicked the water and pulled at its imaginary strings. Out of breath and coughing, we made it to the surface at the muddy shore. And choking with teary eyes, we laughed out heartily at how easy it had been. We would then control our breaths and slowly start swimming, learning and trying out new skills each other day. Sometimes we held our friends' hands and told them to kick, slowly letting them go as we watched them float away, and when they heard our voices from a distance, they fumbled and tumbled a little.

When the girls saw us swimming, impressed, they made fun of our bony bodies and then asked us to teach them, and we smiled at our secret wonder. They would hide to remove the skirts and dresses and return dressed in long petticoats with tiny straps at the shoulders. We saw their breasts peeking through their underwear, and our chests heaved. We instructed them on how to swim while holding on to the jerrycans, the feel of their skin most welcome in the freezing water. Sometimes they tumbled over the jerrycans and, fidgeting and grabbing around, grazed their hands against our already hard manhoods under the water. After that, they sometimes fidgeted more intently, holding on to our manhoods a little longer, and our hands would press their breasts a little more surely.

Once our bodies were no longer dark blue silhouettes and started taking on clearer shades of black and brown, the girls got out of the stream. We would swim a little more to kill our embarrassments, then go fill our jerrycans at the rocky parts of the stream, the water gushing out in powerful white thrusts to quickly fill them.

Afterwards, we scouted the palm oil trees to see if any were ripe for plucking in the evening when the trees were warmer and softer, then took the water home before running to school.

It was on one such morning that we found them, strangers to the village. They were there before us, and we feared they would spoil our sport. They had tape measures and little books in their hands and told us not to worry they only wanted to bring a machine. They said that they would bring piped water to our homes. We wouldn't have to brave the biting cold to fetch water for our fathers and mothers.

'But our siblings,' we said. 'What shall we do when little Nyanja starts noticing a girl in class? When we can't tell her sister to tell her to go fetch water, and we send him too.'

'The machine,' they replied, 'will transform your lives. Kalisizo will no longer be just a small village in the deep south of the country. It will become a hub of activity. Ask your siblings if they wouldn't want tap water.'

We went back home and told our fathers and mothers. They didn't like the sound of a machine, but their backs were worn out, they said.

We asked our siblings if they minded the machine.

Our little siblings, who still only woke if they felt the sun's fingers touch their eyelids when they turned both left and right, replied, 'That sounds wonderful.'

'Shall we be able to fish from the stream?' our little siblings asked us.

'They say we shall,' we replied.

'Sounds amazing. Progress and modernization are the way,' our little siblings said.

The machine came slowly. It was slithered through our Kalisizo, spiking some curiosity. A little optimism here and a little pessimism there. 'It was just a machine. What could it do?' some said. And slowly, every other morning, we found it larger, a little longer, like a python that has just swallowed a calf.

We still went to the stream. We were now a little too old to swim at dawn, so we went for the palm oil. The trees grew around the swamp in an assortment of tribes. The palm oil trees grew tall without branches, and we would look up and see the red and orange fruits nestled on the trunk below the crown of green leaves. With our feet and knees and hands, we climbed the brown and green trunks and, when we reached the apex, plucked the little fruits, throwing them down for those on the ground to collect. If the fruits were nearer, we let our younger brothers harvest them.

Miti, despite being younger than us, was tall and wide, his hands spreading out like proud branches. He always climbed and plucked every last ripe fruit from a tree.

Ignoring the hum of the machine, we would sit under the trees and peel the red skins off the little fruits, then eat the fatty yellow-fibred fruit like in the days before the machine. We ate until our mouths were buttery and our lips itched like caterpillars had crawled over them. Sometimes we took the fruits home and boiled them, creating creamy oil that we kept in empty tins and cooked with.

The machine, too, was an eater. First, they brought the things it needed in large trucks, raw materials to make the things they said we needed. Then it started eating around. It started with the trees. It was for our own good, they said. So it ate them, large chunks at a time, and the forests around the stream started balding in large patches. The machine was a machine; it didn't know which trees were young and which were old, which tree had ripe fruit and which had raw fruit, which tree housed the shy birds and which didn't. It ate them all.

The machine was growing bigger. It needed more raw materials, more space, more labour. It started calling our younger siblings, employing them. Miti was the first to go. He walked into the machine and came back after ten hours. We were alarmed, but he needed the work. The new jobs were fairly profitable. The next day he spent twelve hours, and we said no, but the machine needed the labour. The next time he walked into the machine, he never came back. We waited for Miti, but he was gone. We asked at the machine, and they said they had too much to do. They had too many workers. We needed to write letters showing 'probable cause' and explaining why he was lost or why we thought the machine had taken him. We went home.

But our fathers, broken, pitched at the machine. Unwilling to move until they heard about him.

'Miti, burly, with arms large like proud branches,' they asked.

'Miti who stands when the winds get too strong. A man of his word,' they asked.

'What do you think we could ever do without our son?' our fathers implored, and they were ignored. The machine was too big for them. Quietly, powerless, our fathers came back home. Their backs bent a little more.

The machine kept growing bigger. They filled half the swamp with soil to give it more land, the trees no longer in the way. It was a spoilt child, an insatiable emperor, needing and wanting more under the guise of benevolence.

'Why?' we asked the bringers of the machine. 'Isn't there another way?'

'Yes,' they replied, 'but it would be more expensive.'

'What could be more expensive than this?' we wondered, not recognising the place that had built our childhood and teenage years. The place of wonder, of swimming and fishing, of fruit and water.

When we were younger, we went to the stream to fish. This was before the machine began emptying its dirt and oils into the swamp, before the fish started floating on the water. The machine had become a smoking, shitting man. It released white and grey fumes into the sky and excreted black mucky oils into the swamp.

When we went fishing, we waded through the swamp to the rotting logs and clumps of papyrus in which the mudfish lived. With sharp eyes and quick hands, we seized what we could before the fish glided under the muddy water. We made fun of those that had failed to get any, for we each had our bad day. Everyone but little Nyanja. His were telescopic eyes and magnetic hands. When he spotted the fish, he sharply grabbed it and set it wiggling aside, and immediately caught another. He knew he owned the fishes and walked with the wind at his back. He walked with the softness and hardness of the sea. After we caught enough, we stacked the mudfish onto sticks and took them home, sun-dried them, then smoked them. Afterwards, we either sold them or gave them to our mothers to put in the binyebwa sauce.

We knew that the days of Nyanja as the king of the fishes were growing shorter, the dusks falling quicker. See, the machine was greedy. It churned and ground, day and night. Like a glutton without any spittle left to push down the food, the machine grabbed the water next. First, it sucked from the underground. Different waters, they said. But maybe it loved the taste of water, for it sucked the last of the swamp, then the stream. It sucked them up like it was using a straw. We protested, but the machine was now too big to hear us. It was a giant we couldn't see the end of, a white and silver, steel and concrete beast.

We told Nyanja and our other younger siblings of the days of the shy, gentle sun, for we now woke with the sun burning our eyes. We told them of the places at the stream where we found our spouses under the covers of mist and fog.

'Where shall you find wives?' we asked.

'Those were your days. Imagine braving such biting cold just to find a wife,' our siblings replied.

'Where shall you find husbands?' we asked.

'At the machine. It's where all young people work and interact. We shall find husbands there.'

Nyanja disappeared slowly. Receding slowly into his body. Slowly he lost the winds at his back, for whenever he went to the machine, he came back less. It was hard for us to notice because we lived with him. We saw him every day. But when an aunt would visit, disturbed, she would ask, 'What happened to Nyanja? He has lost his body.'

'He goes to the machine to look for a wife. Maybe it tires him,' we would answer.

Then we started to notice, too, for it was impossible to miss. But by then, it was too late. He receded into his body until he went to the machine and never came back.

Aggrieved, we went to the machine. We looked at its high gates and turned back home.

But our mothers, not letting go of the beautiful son, stood by the gates and asked, 'Have you seen Nyanja, who owns the fishes?'

The machine did not answer.

'Is Nyanja here, he who walks with the breeze at his back?'

The machine swallowed its voice.

Broken, their eyes sunken, our mothers came back home, with fresh grief in their gaits.

We looked at Nkuba, our little princess. She who filled our lives with smiles, a blessing of old age to our fathers and mothers. Nkuba, who would show up while we worked in the garden with a cup of water for each of us. Nkuba, who brought sudden unexpected laughter. We looked at her, looked at our fathers and mothers, and promised to protect her. The machine would not take her.

We protected Nkuba. We prayed for her. We laid sacrifices for her. We formed rings around her. Unfailingly, the machine pursued her. It seduced her with mumbled promises. It hummed her name with its metallic voice.

'What's here for me? Why not let me go?' Nkuba asked, 'Our lives revolve around the machine now.'

And in reply, we did the little we could to make her happy. We sent her around less; we worked with what she gave us.

But she did not see it.

'Just hold on a little,' we begged her.

'What do you need me for?' she asked. 'You don't go to the garden anymore.'

'Please, Nkuba, try to understand,' we pleaded.

See, in the older days, we knew when it was time to plant. We knew when the rains would fall. We knew when the sun would shine. Before the season of the rain, we would till the soil, dark earth that smelt of fresh rot, still a little hard because the land had been at rest. During those seasons, we woke up before the sun melted the fog into tiny drops of dew. When the younger ones went to the stream, we went to the garden. When the first light rains fell, we planted, our hoes swinging from morning to late evening, acre after acre. When we were done, we wiped the sweat off our dark clenched brows, sat under tree shades and looked proudly at the work of our hands. We sent Nkuba for our dinner of matooke and fresh beans, sometimes cassava if we had worked too hard, and made fruitful predictions about harvests while we ate.

How could we tell her it was more than the digging for us? It was the blessing. It was the laughter she brought. And how would we go to the gardens now? The hoes broke in the hardened soil, for the sun now shined with no shame in its nakedness. The soil was littered with pellets of plastic from the machine. How could we sort those out before they choked anything we attempted to grow? We could not go to the garden, we said, with no trees to rest under after. They are all fallen and dry. We wouldn't know when it would be time to plant; the lakes and swamps had long dried up and no longer gave warning breezes. Sometimes the rain came sparsely, like an afterthought, a spray that left us thirstier than before. Other times it came saying it wouldn't be back for a long time, so it showered for weeks on end. First, it filled the containers we left to collect the rainwater, for we could not tell when next it'd rain and the taps often ran dry. Then it filled the rivulets it dug itself, but they led nowhere; the swamp and stream were no longer home. So, it filled the land and then our houses. We couldn't go to the gardens.

'Your brothers,' we would ask Nkuba, 'do you still remember them?'

She would look at us and smile. And we felt she understood.

But Nkuba was hot and cold those days. She would lose her temper and tear up harshly and then recoil into herself. She gave us her laughter now so rarely. Whenever she recoiled into herself, she would go to the machine and not tell us. We would keep waiting, and suddenly she would show up.

We never realised Nkuba had been taken. We waited until we knew.

We went to the machine. We carried our fathers' brokenness in our hearts. We carried our mothers' grief.

We did not ask about her at the machine.

We did not ask for Nkuba.

We did not ask about her, who brought sudden unexpected laughter.

We went at night. With our hands, we started to scratch at the concrete walls. With our hands, bare and bleeding, we tore at the steel. We plucked pieces off the giant and disposed of them. We dismantled the machine throughout the night. The machine was large; we could not see the end of it, but we kept pulling, digging and uprooting all that was hidden under the ground.

Here we were, once boys and girls of the stream. Once at this hour, frolicking in icy waters, now warring with a strange beast. Then more people came and dismantled with us. Our backs ached and bent, some broke, but we kept going. Some got tired and went home, saying it was just too big, we couldn't break it all down. But we kept going, losing track of time.

The morning came early, for mist and fog were a thing of the past. With the sun came armies that surrounded us. Criminals, they called us, speaking through black metal masks, their bodies covered from head to toe in dark heavy armaments. Clubs slung from their bodies; heavy guns swung in their hands. We looked at our bloody hands and asked, 'Don't you have siblings? Didn't the machine take them never to return?'

The armies did not answer. They marched on. With their clubs they hit us. And yet we continued to break the machine. Dismantling the hundreds of its joints, the thousands of its screws. They arrested us. They sentenced us. They continued to hit us. They broke our legs. They broke our arms. Those of us that survived continued breaking and dismantling the machine. Tearing down its concrete walls that now lay in rubble all around us. Then they started shooting, an end for some of the most valorous. We did not look back, left or right. We kept on ravaging the monster, for what use was it to live today and be taken away tomorrow. Then the machine was falling, dust rising in its stead. We looked around, and we were all covered in dust. We couldn't tell who the armies were, for everyone was covered in the white dust of the falling machine. In the confusion, the strangers disappeared, abandoning their invention. But weary we were of the eating shitting machine, so we kept going. When we stopped, the machine kept crashing down, its metals molten.

Some claim they missed the hum of the machine, for it had been here for ages. Children had been born and raised with its sound. Others had missed the silence of the village, but it was simply the memory, for when the silence returned, its beauty was new to us all.

In the silence, with rich dark clouds hovering above, Nyanja was the first we saw. Faint, a frame at a distance, he staggered on, getting bigger and steadier the closer he came. He had the winds at his back, moving as soft and as hard as the sea.

CITIZEN SARAH
Fayssal Bensalah

Possibly all staff members of Parisian hotels regale about haunted rooms and prominent guests, except at *Hôtel Bastille*, whose employees—and occasionally guests too—still wonder about the distinct glasses of the manager. I still do, when alone, when in the company of my co-workers. The glasses are a pince-nez, without earpieces, a brand, or a relation to our twenty-first century. Just a duo of glass discs, round and misty, united with a silver wire. They are also, I must emphasise, cracked: two lines almost split each lens. Has he—we sometimes ask—purchased them from a memorabilia shop on Rue Frantz Fanon or Rue Hélène Andras?

Perhaps, for their outmoded frames refuse to remain locked against his nasal bones, constantly sliding to the tip of his nose, leading to an inconvenient habit. He, to replace them, compulsively pushes them up with his thumb when managing his establishment, when being himself. Has he inherited them from a relative or an army officer? Could be, our speculation goes, but only their wearer knows for certain, the manager of *Hôtel Bastille* himself—Monsieur F. Jules.

Mr Jules isn't a male model. But he enjoys posing anywhere he pleases, anywhere. He is another pillar of the hotel, a mobile one. It puzzles us, we his underlings; it keeps us alarmed, awake, industrious. It caffeinates us. Do his eyes tail us behind the lenses? Is he watching us constantly? Or asleep?

Are his eyes thorough or selective?

He hides—that's the source of his power.

Is Mr Jules blind? Those who've seen his eyes state, reassure, that he is not. Trust me. I know. I am the concierge of the hotel, Mademoiselle Miriam Pascal, who's been closely in service with him for eleven years and thus has enjoyed exposure to his eyes.

Is he allergic to light? That's a plausible presumption, for I have noted squiggly lines surface on Jules' eyes, scarlet as the stigmas of saffron, as if they were imperial tenacles sprouting from his pupils and colonising his eyes. In fact, I witness them again this evening as I urgently pinpoint him by the elevators in the lobby and notify him of an issue in the lounge. I, edgy, growing sweaty, knead my hands together while Jules's eyes pulse at me from behind the twin lenses. An issue?

'What is it?'

'A hijab affair.'

It is late evening. It is the hour of jazzy music. It is the season of honeymooners in our hotel, whose lobby still receives tardy lovers returning from soirées, from intimate conversations on benches. A synthetic scent, a warm one that touches everything, even pores, fills the atmosphere. It streams from the circular lounge where four leathery, quilted sofas face one another underneath a crystal chandelier. Its scintillating light enlivens the entire hotel, the boulevard, Paris. But, apparently, not the assaulted lady.

Saturated by its gleam, suspended on one of the sofas, the hijabi lady quivers, still shaken. She whimpers sporadically, especially after her husband, a bearded man, feels the bruises on her face.

There, an hour ago, Mr Jules struck the gong three times, a yearly tradition that announces the season of honeymooners. As his staff members flanked him, including myself, including the sixty-year-old doorman, Mr Jules soaked the cosy lounge with resonant tunes, declaring *Hôtel Bastille* a nest of lovers for a month. A brief speech followed, a series of rigorous orders. Be cordial. No issues, you hear? I didn't hear; I was gazing at the cracks in his glasses. Were they dilating? His hair is greying along the sides, a few loyal guests have commented, still notice. And so do I as I now stand on heels in front of him, with an embroidered cravat around my neck. An accessory to identify my role at the hotel. Jules removes his fingers from the elevator's push button and asks: 'What's happened?'

I predict his response. He's trained me. To assess the situation, we stride to the lounge in tandem. Jules greets and bows his head to our guests rather carefully so he won't drop the glasses. He seeks the maintenance of the peace. The euphoric mood must not be alarmed. A couple of honeymooners traipsing past us flirt, giggle. They promise wild nights, no sleep. I overhear them as I stand next to Mr Jules, who, without a word, regards the hijabi lady from a long distance. They can't see us; we can see them. The brown back of the sofa can be seen, and three heads. Only one of them trembling. Only one half covered with a scarf.

The husband is still soothing his wife, now with the assistance of a third person. A blonde woman is with the Muslim couple; she's offering them a bottle of water, a few tissues, even words: *C'est inacceptable! Que s'est-il passé?*

'Is she a guest of the hotel?' Mr Jules says, pushing his glasses up with his thumb. 'Is she one of our honeymooners?'

'I think so.'

'Be certain,' he says. 'Check.'

I wish not to unease them further. I've already done so when the matter was brought to my attention. I leave my heels with Mr Jules and tiptoe to the sofa. Hello again, I say, how are we? The Muslim lady is unable to collect herself, is unable to respond to her husband's attempts at comforting, to his sedative words: you're safe now; I am here. He kneels in front of her, his face dry, his hands tender on her face.

She's still rigid on the sofa, breathing asthmatically into her hair, slightly tousled as if it's been yanked. Her left cheek is grazed as if rubbed with nails. Her man is trying to tighten her scarf around her hair, replace it, but he's doing a terrible job.

His wife closes her eyes, not wanting to see him.

I don't want to seem indelicate or officious, but I need to do my job. I have questions, and Mr Jules is watching. I sit at the far end of the sofa, tuck my feet together, wait for a thoughtful moment. The Muslim lady is empty of words, rich with faint groans. She shuts herself. But Mr Jules is watching, impatient for answers, for the inception of a resolution.

So I ask his questions: Madame, are you guests of the hotel? Are you one of our newlyweds? Can you hear me?

'*Ce n'est pas possible!*' the blonde lady says to me, a bit annoyed. 'She needs to be examined by a doctor. Do something. Call the police. Do something.'

'It's protocol, Madame.'

I look up at Mr Jules, who reads my failure at once. The heels are gone, taken no doubt by a lobby attendant. I see the manager, impassive, still waiting. This is Mr Jules—forty-four, overweight as an uncle. As usual, he wears his uniform, his blue navy suit. He stands like a magistrate, chin up, chest out, shoulders back. An unnatural pose that aches his back. I, at times, catch his groans. This pose protrudes his rosy cheeks, which highlights his glasses, two round buttons lost in a doughy face. He remains erect, even when he raises his fingers to his lips now, and twirls an imaginary moustache, referring to Mr Mustafa, our North African doorman, who might have witnessed the potential assault.

Mr Mustafa Harkè doffs the terrible bowler hat that we force him to wear when the hotel's automatic door hisses open, revealing me. The hat is unfashionable, of course, outdated. But it serves a purpose. It's a nostalgia bait. Our guests love it. Besides, it suits the doorman's brush-like moustache. The elegant North African rarely partakes in conversation with our guests. His job, you see, is lonely, is solitary. It engulfs him with silence.

'A hijabi lady was assaulted?' he says, touching the rim of his hat. 'Umm, which one?'

'I was hoping you could tell me.'

'The night isn't young.'

'She's in our lounge, in a terrible state.'

'Our lounge? It's not my place to say, Mademoiselle,' he says, inspecting the boulevard. 'I smile. I greet, I open the door, and I usher. I see nothing. But Mr Jules does. You ought to ask him.'

I return to the manager. Although Jules occupies a position of power, he isn't stern or assertive. Far from it. He's delicate, fickle. A parent of his, we often joke, owns the hotel, which scored him the position. He suffers from his fleshy weight; it damages his breath. He tires easily, which is why he's currently sitting on a stool borrowed from the minibar, the dough of his lower body swallowing the seat. Mr Jules's eyes are still glued to the Muslim woman.

'Mr Mustafa didn't witness the assault.'

'No, he didn't,' Jules says. 'He smiles, he greets, he opens the door, and he ushers. He sees nothing.'

There are other ways to find out, Mr Jules says. I improvise. A lobby attendant brings my tablet from my desk. I tap its screen, searching for the guest list, for their scanned passports. Our app saves our guests' pictures too, even their ages, even their addresses. Her name must be Arabic-sounding or Muslim-sounding. I try Jamila, Fatima, Nadifa and such. I know these names; I grew up in Marseille, where a large community of Muslims thrive, where I'd overhear such names. I find it. It's . . . neutral. It's Sarah. I see her face, different, natural, happy. Is that really her in the lounge?

'Mr Jules, she's one of our guests,' I say, at last. 'She's one of our honeymooners. We should check the CCTV cameras. If the assault took place near the entrance of the hotel, they would certainly have the recording. Should I call the operator of the hotel's CCTV cameras, Bohai? Should we call the police now? I'll call Bohai. He never sleeps.'

'I know who Bohai is,' Mr Jules says. 'You're making decisions on my behalf now, Mademoiselle?'

'I dare not, Monsieur.'

'This is what I want you to do,' he says, feeling the bridge of his glasses with a finger. 'Check her passport again, know where she's from and call her embassy. They'll collect her and her husband. It's their job, you see? And provide them with some refreshments when they arrive for her. I wouldn't want them to think us inhospitable.'

'But Monsieur Jules,' I say, 'she's a French citizen.'

None of our honeymooners has visited my desk. They're lost in each other. Is Mr Jules, too? Lost in himself? He is inactive on the stool. I am still standing next to him, next to his cryptic silences. I don't like this. It's late evening, and I am tired of episodic incidents at the hotel, like this one. It's protracting. I am tired of asking Mr Jules's questions. Let him run his own errands. Let him ask his own questions. I can't endure silence and inactivity as he does. I am not a pillar of the hotel. Should I nudge him? Is he sleeping? No, he isn't. I hear his heavy breaths, produced with difficulty. What is he waiting for? The—

'Barbarians,' he says. 'Look at her. She's lying on our sofa without removing her shoes.'

Sarah curls on the sofa, curls around herself, around her increasing silence, like a leaf. Her husband is clueless, walking in circles, doubting himself, eying his lady with uncertainty. He checks his surroundings. Honeymooners are still enjoying themselves at the minibar, self-serving shot after shot. He's an invisible man. I think he may scream, kick our furniture, or just self-explode. Being a husband is a novel experience to him, it seems to me. Is Mr Jules watching this?

I don't know.

I can't see his eyes.

That's his power—he hides.

'Mademoiselle Pascal,' Mr Jules says, 'you better subdue him before he makes a scene.'

It is not he who may make a scene, but the blonde woman, passionately thin, tenacious, still benevolent to the Muslim couple. Who is she? She slaps Sarah's husband on the shoulder with the back of her hand, an impatient reproach, and tells him to pull his shit together. She aims again, but he dodges it, kneeling in front of his wife's face. I am by the sofa, Sarah's sneakers touching my feet. I think touching his wife in our presence embarrasses him, though he realises her urgent need for it, so he employs comforting words again. Sarah responds, leaving her trauma for a moment, briefly but enough to crack her husband.

She murmurs, 'How could you let this happen?'

Sarah's husband does not stagger, gasp, or gather his pieces. Down there, facing his wife, he growls, with an open mouth, not at her, not at us, at no one, at nothing. He stands up and, as if devoid of energy and air, slowly leaves our hotel. Leaves his wife with us. I wish to consult with Mr Jules about this development. I peer for one of his instructive gestures, an order, but pause. The manager abandons his high stool theatrically, adjusts the round shields, and at last, strides towards us, swinging his arms.

'Are you a guest of the hotel?' he says, not specifying to whom. 'Are you?'

I am unsure about his intentions. But he is my leader, my superior, my employer. I am a passive viewer. Mr Jules laces his hands behind his back, inflates his chest ostentatiously like a rooster. Is he about to crow? To rouse Sarah from her trauma? It appears so; he's facing her, after all, gazing at her as if about to perform an exorcism. His twin discs pass over her in ominous silence.

It is the first time he exposes his eyes publicly, not caring about the blonde lady standing next to me or anyone who might wander into our party of three. Mr Jules reaches for his glasses, for their silver bridge, with his thumb and index finger, delicately as if it were a crust or a straw. He removes them. He doesn't part with them, his precious glasses, not pocketing them, not saving them in a case. They remain caught in his adamant grip. An attractive accessory.

I see his eyes, intoxicated with insomnia, with looming collapse. They're throbbing. Do they hide tiny hearts? They're damp. I see them as a duet of unripe radishes, with pulsing roots, racing towards his pupils like sperms.

Sarah is still a cocoon. The sofa accommodates her entirely. So does her hijab, which envelopes her, which veils the shape of her body. She breathes softly like a baby at dawn. The marks on her face are still there, still scratched. Citizen Sarah, where are you? Emerge. Open up, glare at your bully. Speak up.

I am a spectator; my job demands it. I follow Mr Jules. The blonde lady, however, after minutes of confusion and now astonishment, speaks against Mr Jules's histrionics, against his cryptic silences.

'What's this?' she says, eying us both incredulously, disoriented. 'What are you doing?'

'I am probing for the truth,' Mr Jules says, ignoring her indignant gaze. 'The truth has certain signs on a person's face. Experience and training teach me to recognise the signs.'

'What truth?' she says. 'This woman needs help. Look at her. She's been attacked. Her husband is alienated. Your inaction shocks me. All you do is watch. What's going on here?'

'Are you her advocate?'

'I am a French woman.'

'Madame, I realise—'

'Do you, Joll?'

'It's Jules,' he says. 'It's Mr Jules to you.'

'I am calling the police.'

'You will not do such a thing if you know what's good for you,' Mr Jules says, not looking at her. 'You have no power here. I am the manager. I am the decision maker. Are you, by the way, a guest at our hotel?'

'That's irrelevant.'

'I don't remember you at the check-in queue,' he says. 'And you're alone. You're not one of our honeymooners. You've come here for a drink at our bar. I've seen you. I am afraid you're trespassing on our hospitality, Madame.'

'You're kicking me out? Oh, you'll hear from me, Mr Joll,' she says. A purse is by the sofa. The blonde lady yanks it, wears one of its straps around her arms. Then she smiles at Sarah and leaves through the revolving doors.

Citizen Sarah leaves her trance just then, with virtue, with deference. Her emergence, her unfolding, undergoes three phases. A sigh, first, a courteous breath. A sitting position, second, a dignified one. Then, third, a scarf adjustment. The piece of cloth, blue as her republic's flag, doesn't secure her hair. It seeps onto her shoulders. Gracefully, with experienced hands, she seizes its hems and envelopes her hair. It bundles it. This is a meticulous operation, artful, even artistic. She then tucks a few wild hairs into the piece of clothing with four fingers. She winces when touching her face's fresh scars. Then she relaxes, then she livens up.

This, to me, is a normal operation, performed daily and commonly as wearing a shirt, a top, a blazer, a coat, a hat, any piece of clothing. To Mr Jules, however, it is terror. It is defiance. It is an unlawful view, an encroachment on the values of the hotel. The cracks in his glasses dilate, almost splitting the lenses. He's about to erupt, to pour loud words into the lounge.

Citizen Sarah speaks. Sarah moves her lips. Before she assembles her belongings, before she locates her hotel room key, before she ambles towards the elevators and nestles in her room, she tells Mr Jules, 'You will fall. Like an empire, you will fall.'

Monsieur F. Jules feels naked without the glasses. He wears them with all possible haste. He sets them on the bridge of his nose and pushes them against it with his index finger and thumb, hard enough to dent his nose, cause a red mark. He does it three, four, five times. Obsessively. Almost paranoidly. They refuse to remain in their ordinary place, repeatedly gliding like a loose switch button, down, up, down, up. As a solution, he abandons the thumb and uses the index finger to suspend the glasses before his face, pressing it against the bridge of the twin discs. He breathes steadily now, with his index finger pinned to his face as if pointing at himself.

One index finger.

Mr Harkè is waving in the lobby. He presses his hat to his chest and waits to meet Mr Jules' eyes. No guest is roaming the lobby or walking on the red carpet, none leaving, none entering. The honeymooners are spent in their bedrooms, entangled in each other and won't emerge until midday tomorrow. Only the staff members recline drowsily on bannisters, doors and counters. The experienced doorman knows his craft as he paints a smile on his moustached face and becomes a hermit, wishing not to disturb the peace of the hotel. He waves again, then reinstates himself at his post outside.

'Mr Jules?' I say.

'Follow me.'

Our hotel's steps are submerged in blue lights. A police car has parked in the vicinity of the establishment. Fortunately, the boulevard had quieted, free of noise, except the humming of the light poles, of the moon, and of the cuffed man. That's what Mr Jules does first when he sees the police car; he scans the perimeter, which promises an unwelcome concern.

'What is it, Mr Mustafa?' Mr Jules says. 'Speak now.'

'A terror, Mr Jules,' the doorman says. 'A barbarian.'

About a few meters down the street, the man is cuffed around an unlit pole, cushioning a few trash bags. It is Sarah's husband. He is on the wet pavement, trying to wrestle himself free. A tenuous protest, futile, but he keeps doing it, growling like an engine. He's trying to kick the boots of the three police officers who've arrested him, two of whom are now approaching us.

They don't ask their questions yet. They don't enforce their inquiries. They push their fingers into their belts and open their mouths, but Mr Mustafa beats them to it and acts unlike himself. He spits words, many of them, not onto them, but onto Mr Jules.

'It was him. He was terrorising the pedestrians,' the night doorman says. 'He grabbed their shirts, screaming, "Was it you? Was it you?" I heard him. I saw everything. He's a mad one. He's a violent one, Mr Jules. I witnessed this. He should be detained. He's a barbarian, Mr Jules. He should not be part of our republic.'

'He's right,' one of the officers says. 'The suspect stopped people on the street and started shouting in their faces, "Was it you? Was it you?" We found a hotel door card on him that has this hotel's name on it. *Was it you?* Do you know anything about that, Mr . . . ?'

'Do you not see the glasses?' Mr Jules says.

Mr Jules steers the two police officers down the street, where they mutter as if disinterested in the incident. I close my eyes and wait. Sarah's husband, one of our honeymooners, calls my name. He's calmed down; I approach him cautiously. Someone should wipe his nose and lips clean; they're soaping with spittle and tears. There are glitters of sanity on him, seeming innocent and warm. His spine is arched, which pressures his lungs. He can't breathe naturally, can't look up at me when he sees my feet before him.

'How's my wife?' he coughs.

'She's fine, ' I say. 'She's in her room now.'

It relieves him. He's a cold flame. Sarah's husband sits in disgrace, in the company of the trash bags, collecting his fragments as if he were a mutinous soldier. When he pulls a breath to uphold his life, his upper body jerks upwards, which forces friction between the cuffs and the pole. He coughs and doesn't blink, not even when I pat him on the shoulder. Once, twice, before he shrugs me off.

'Was it you, Mademoiselle?' he says.

Then he lowers his head further and waits as if for the guillotine. Mr Jules and the officers are still huddled together, speaking. The suspect is a man of questions. He murmurs other ones, he exhales them. I listen.

'Where would we go?' he says, not particularly to me.

The night is wheeling slowly. But no worries, hotels don't sleep. Our hotel certainly doesn't. I remove my blazer and cover his shoulders and cuffed wrists. There, there. He doesn't recoil. He doesn't resist.

Later, when Sarah unshuts, she will confide in me. I will listen. She will also share miserable words: scarf, the attacker, his motorcycle, the slurs, the Muslim bitch, the scarf pulling, the fall, the Muslim bitch again, the dragging, the screams, the tears, the shock, the husband running across the street from a shop to find his wife on the pavement, then his shock, then cradling his wife into the hotel, into our lounge.

She will share that she's a local. She was born in Paris twenty-five years ago. Her father, Claude, now retired, was the manager of a Renault car factory, which has prospered during his tenure. Madeline, her mother, is a paediatrician in Paris, credited with preventing premature funerals, appreciated for relieving parents. Sarah has a brother who's managed to play for the French football team and score a few winning goals.

Sarah is an online educator. She converted to Islam at the age of sixteen. A high-school friend, a Muslim, introduced her to it. Yes, many eyebrows were raised, many concerns, even threats. The parents still call her daughter, still open the door for her when she visits. So does her brother, who's befriended a few Muslim players on the field. She's lost a few friends, however. Others have criticised her severely, attacked her with silence. It's a free country, she would answer when asked about it, isn't it? *Liberté, égalité et fraternité,* or have you forgotten the values of our republic?

Have you?

GREY IS A COLOUR THAT NEVER STAINS
Ani Kayode Somtochukwu

There, under the Kuka tree,
his shoes billow, hanging by their worn laces.
Their colours fade, slowly, ever so slowly
like the dying sunset,
or the whipping wind,
which, after the rains,
became an ordinary country breeze.

Today, like all other days since he lost Harrison, Tobe crawls into bed wearing two pairs of stockings. The first one, a white pair that has dulled to beige, is long and thick and hugs his thighs firmly. The second pair, which only goes past his ankles, is thinner, but together, they provide enough warmth. The air conditioner is turned low to a freezing temperature, misting up the windows and the mirror installed into the wardrobe door. In the morning, the condensation would roll down the glass in small droplets. The AC and what temperature it should be turned to used to be such a contentious topic. Tobe liked his AC turned to a rational 20 or 21 degrees, but Harrison preferred it so low that Tobe would start losing feeling in the tip of his fingers and toes. Most days, Harrison got his way, and

Tobe would swaddle himself in layers and layers of blankets. Today he uses fewer blankets. In Harrison's absence, he finds that the cold is not that bad. Listening to the harmattan wind whistle against the windowpane, he tries to clear his mind. Before long, he feels it, a hand on his leg, the touch so faint it is barely a shadow. Tears well slowly in his eyes, and when they fall, they are warm against the sides of his face. The hand drifts up his leg, rests on his stomach for a moment before continuing up to the dip of his neck.

'Why?' he thinks to himself. 'Was I not enough?' He whispers this to the shadow, but it is only a fleeting thought. He *knows* why.

The touch fades into the dark, but still, sleep evades Tobe. He lies in the quiet, hoping to feel it again. Then he drifts off with the dark to the huge, weathered flame tree on Douglas Street under which he first met Harrison long ago, back when the fleeting shadow was flesh and bones.

'Seventeen years,' he thinks to himself and turns on his side, pulling the covers to his wet face before readjusting it under his chin. How is it possible to love someone that long and then wake up one day and be expected to live without them? A part of him wanted to apportion blame, to feel betrayed, but Tobe understood more than anyone else how Harrison was a man cracked by circumstance, how shards of broken dreams can cut bone-deep wounds that never heal. In the last days, Tobe felt a hushed reticence growing between them, the intimacy they once shared dulling to estrangement. Tobe hoped and hoped, buoyed by memories of a time when they looked to the future with anticipation, unaware of how cruel this world could be. He dreams of it still: it is 2007, and they are in Tobe's lodge at Parklane. It is raining so heavily that they can barely hear each other speak. They are naked, the doors and windows firmly locked, and the curtains pulled together. Underneath the sheets, they craft a future of their own, untethered by the world beyond that room. Sometimes it is a hazy dream, but the happy comfort,

Tobe always remembers. The fiddling of fingers, the warmth of skin to skin, the salty taste of Harrison's sweat, the weight of Harrison's body on his, the certainty of their shared aspirations. Waking from those dreams, Tobe would stir in bed till sunrise, feeling all choked up, as though on the verge of tears, as though in the middle of an unfinished song.

Harrison loved eating at Cilantro. He loved the low light and the way the wine bottles were hung at the bar and the water fountain and the plants. But he hated that each time a waiter brought the bill, they handed it to Tobe.

Once, on a Saturday evening on which they shared a bottle of Ermelinda Rosé, he called the waiter back and asked, 'Why did you give him the bill?'

The waiter looked at Tobe and then looked back at him. 'Nothing, sir,' he said.

'It can't be nothing. Come on,' Harrison said, laughing. The waiter laughed along but said nothing.

'Get the POS,' Tobe said to diffuse the situation. Harrison was unpredictable when he drank. They took a cab home, and as they trudged into the living room, Harrison stopped suddenly, 'We forgot to tip the waiter.'

'No, I remembered,' Tobe said, manoeuvring past him and onto a sofa. He kicked off his shoes, placed his feet on the centre table. 'I gave him 2k.'

Eventually, the waiters learnt to drop the bill in the middle of the table, from where Harrison would pick it up and look through it while Tobe fished his ATM from his wallet.

The first time he went there alone, the waiter that seated Tobe asked, 'This one you came by yourself, sir.' And it took him by pleasant surprise that he saw them that way, as a pair, even though it shouldn't have. Tobe smiled weakly and mumbled politely, glancing around before dropping his gaze to his lap.

The waiter left, and when he returned, he had two menus in his hands. He placed one before Tobe and then, holding the other with both hands, asked, 'It's like *oga* is still on the way, or it's just you?'

Tobe stared at him and smiled weakly. He picked up his menu, but it trembled in his hands. 'Just me,' he mumbled, dropping the menu and hiding his shaky hands below the table, not having the heart to tell him Harrison died.

Tobe describes meeting Harrison as though it was a rescue. It felt that way, as though his whole life was a series of random meaningless events that all took on meaning after they met.

'You make it sound like you were homeless, and I found you,' Harrison once said.

Tobe was entertaining friends in the living room, and Harrison, not liking any of Tobe's friends, made himself scarce. He only occasionally appeared to rebut something Tobe had said.

'In a way, I was. And you did,' Tobe said and turned towards him.

'We were in SS1, Tobe. Be serious.'

It was not so easy to explain that, even at that age, Tobe was an extremely lonely child, used to being waited on, used to friends who played with him and were nice to him, but with whom he was never really comfortable. Tobe feared that one day, he would wake up and have nobody, not even his siblings. It was with Harrison that, for the first time, he felt at ease.

'How did the both of you even go to the same sch—' one of his friends began to ask, voice keen with a sort of admirational envy. Tobe gave him a dissuading look. But it was too late. Harrison heard and emerged from the kitchen to perch on the arm of a sofa.

'Now what on God's earth do you mean by that question, Francis?'

He had a self-satisfied look on his face like he just found proof of something only he once believed.

'I don't mean it like that,' Francis said.

'How do you mean it?'

'Harrison, please,' Tobe said. 'It's an innocent question.'

Harrison shrugged and went back into the kitchen, leaving an awkward silence behind him.

'What's his problem?' someone whispered, but Tobe already knew Harrison would hold on to this, brandishing it like a weapon. He never particularly liked any of Tobe's friends. Having grown up surrounded by affluence, it took Tobe a long time to figure out how small his friends made Harrison feel, how unimportant. Harrison's dislike was more potent for the friends Tobe made in Lagos, taking on the venom of disdain.

'What is your problem with my friends?' Tobe would ask, feeling unduly attacked. 'It was said in jest,' he would say, or, 'Must you take offence and pick apart every single thing they say because they're friends with Tobenna?'

And then one day Harrison told him, 'They think I'm bush,' and it suddenly made sense, 'your rich friends.'

He said it with so much scorn. *Your rich friends.*

It frightened Tobe to hear Harrison talk like that. Made him doubt if he knew Harrison as well as he thought. Moving to Lagos demanded so much of them, throwing into sharp relief just how different their lives were. Tobe did not mind. He was always willing to help Harrison out if he needed money. To pay for dates, groceries, even send Harrison's sister, Adaku, some money to complete her school fees. But it never occurred to him that this was such an uncomfortable spot for Harrison that something as little as a sugar daddy joke could upset him so much.

Sometimes, in his grief, Tobe cannot help but wonder if Lagos is what destroyed them. If perhaps Harrison's death was etched into the stars the day they arrived in Lagos, eyes liquid with hope.

*

Because Chidi has been asking to meet more of Tobe's friends, Tobe takes him to a birthday party in Ajah. The party, held in the living room of a large AirBnB rental, is brightly lit. There are security guards at the gate, and inside, there are so many familiar faces. Tobe even sees someone from work.

'Did you know Dr Onu was gay?' he asks Chidi.

'Yes, we had a thing once. It wasn't serious sha,' Chidi replies, smiling at his shock.

'You had a thing? For real?'

'Yes,' Chidi laughs, 'Why are you saying it like it's unbelievable?'

They meet a couple of Tobe's friends. To them, Tobe introduces Chidi as 'my guy'. Everyone understands what it means, and they are ecstatic for him. Even Chidi is content to be 'my guy', and it makes Tobe think of Harrison. In spaces like this, Tobe introduced Harrison as boyfriend, partner, relishing the way it lit up Harrison's face. It made him nervous because talk like that could so easily get on camera and get to the wrong ears. But it was a fear he did not mind nursing. A fear Harrison no longer seemed to share or understand. It was isolating, the fact that they used to share the same fears, and now they didn't. Now Harrison published scathing articles and gave interviews to news outlets. It was something Tobe had to accept. In the beginning, it was hard. He called Harrison selfish.

'Maybe,' he said, 'Maybe you don't give a shit about yourself, but what about me? Don't you care what happens to me? Nigeria is not America.'

Harrison scoffed. 'Oh, so we're doing emotional manipulation now?'

'No, you dimwit. You're putting me out there. What about *my* career? I know some of my colleagues who have seen your posts, who know that we live together.'

'Oh, do I make your colleagues uncomfortable?'

'You're not using your head, Harrison.'

'No, you're the one not using your head if you want me to bury myself, my work, for you, for your stupid colleagues.'

'Oh, don't pretend this is about money. You're not the first lawyer to work for a human rights organization. They don't make you sign a non-discretion clause when you start. And for God's sake, you don't need to work there. They don't even pay you well. I make enough money for the two of us. We're fine. You can focus on finding somewhere else.'

'God, you rich people think everything is about money, don't you?' Harrison said, his words rushing, his voice rising.

'You rich people? What the fuck is that supposed to mean?' Tobe shouted back.

'It means I don't fucking need your permission to decide what I want to do with my life,' Harrison said, his voice matching Tobe's. Then, in a lower voice, he added, pointing at Tobe's chest, 'I don't police what you can and can't do with your own career. This is me, take it or leave it.'

For days after that, they did not speak, somehow managing to stay out of each other's way in the flat. It was Harrison who broke one Saturday, apologizing for all the words he should not have said. 'This is who I am now. I could never go back to that person who struggled with loving himself, who felt the need to always hide.'

'But you don't need to prove your love for yourself to anyone, certainly not to this godforsaken country. They don't give a fuck, Harrison. If you're killed tomorrow, Nigeria will not pause.'

Harrison sighed. 'Once upon a time, in 1987, a very handsome boy was born.'

'Are you seriously doing a story about yourself?' Tobe chuckled.

'Don't interrupt *nau*,' Harrison said and nudged him.

'Don't remind me how old we are. Omo,' Tobe pressed on, laughing a little, the tension between them thawing.

'Okay, I'll keep my story then,' Harrison said and theatrically folded his hands.

'Ngwa sorry, sorry,' Tobe said. 'Oya what happened to this very handsome boy?'

'The handsome boy grew up feeling weird without knowing why. For years and years, he felt unworthy. One day, he thought he had found a solution: to run to a place that would allow him to flourish so that he could learn how to love himself. But none of that worked out because the people in charge of those places kept rejecting him. He had to learn to love himself regardless. But the problem is, we cannot truly love ourselves in a society that hates us. And so, the only way to love himself became to assert his right to a society that loved him,' he said, his voice quieter at the end. 'If we keep sacrificing ourselves for the promise of safety, we will never get to live in a world where we are safe. All that remained was for this man whom he loved with every fibre of his being to accept him this way, too, without shame.'

Tobe stared at him with mellowed eyes. He wanted to say, *I accept you without shame*, but it sounded outlandishly corny. So, he kissed Harrison instead, to show him that he understood, that all was forgiven. It was the two of them against everything else. Tobe and Harrison.

'I love you too,' Tobe said.

'With every fibre of your being?'

Tobe laughed. 'Yes,' he said, 'with every fibre of my being.'

Now, looking at Chidi, Tobe realizes he will never again be able to love someone that deeply.

Harrison used to be a very quiet boy. The type to avoid provocation, the type that wouldn't confront someone even if they stepped on him. His uncles would joke that it was because he was raised by his mother.

'A boy raised without a father; how will he know to stand up for himself? He's like a woman because a woman raised him.'

Growing up as the first child, he felt saddled with the responsibility of impressing a mother who was very hardly impressed. He strived always to get even higher grades than his last; it did not matter that he was already top of the class. He spent all his spare time reading. He had to be a lawyer, he had to make his mother proud, and he had to show the world. Maybe then he would feel himself worthy. Of what? He was not sure.

In university, he began to shed his shyness, but even then, he never really wanted to be on anybody's bad side. He so quickly agreed for the sake of peace, so easily inconvenienced himself to ingratiate.

The anger he had towards the end of his life was something he learnt as he realized how committed the world was to stamping him out. It was unbelievable to Tobe sometimes how the boy he knew grew into a man who did not want anyone to even make the mistake of assuming he was heterosexual. The boy who used to want, above all else, to fit in, to be approved of. Once, a male coursemate asked him out, and he fidgeted about it for so long Tobe worried he was losing sleep.

'But don't you see?' Harrison said. 'If he sees me like that, that must be what many other people think of me.'

'You're probably overreacting. It's just one person that likes you.'

But he fretted anyway. He told the boy he wasn't like that. No judgement, but he wasn't like that. It is ironic how it was he who used to seek out secrecy, he who reached for door bolts, who locked the windows, drew the curtain as though someone outside might open the windows and raise the curtains. Tobe would watch him walk around the room, making sure everything was locked.

'You should have gotten a first or second-floor room,' Harrison said one day. 'Ground floor room is dangerous. This window is glass. Anyone can break it at any time?'

'Why would anyone just randomly break my window?' Tobe asked, amused.

Harrison rolled his eyes and ignored him. Later, as he made to leave for his hostel, Tobe held his waist. 'Are you angry at me?' he asked, peering into his face.

'No,' Harrison said, still frowning.

'You're being cold,' Tobe pressed on.

'Sometimes when I'm telling you something, you act as if I'm insane.'

Tobe tried not to laugh. 'It's not like that,' he said. 'It's just you worry too much. Nobody is coming in here. No one is going to break my window while we're fucking. Come on.'

Harrison shrugged off Tobe's hands. 'Why? Do you have special anointing that protects you from Nigeria?'

This time Tobe laughed, but Harrison did not find it funny. It did not help that Harrison knew people who had been kitoed, one of whom had his window broken precisely while he was having sex, and Tobe did not, not even one person.

'I'll call you when I get back to UNEC,' he said, and Tobe watched him leave.

It was there, in university, that Harrison first conceived of his escape, one he nursed with a rigid faith. He believed, truly believed, that he'd make his way out of Nigeria. It was something of a religion for him. At the back of his lecture notebook, he made a list of all the schools he would apply to and what their application fees were, in pounds and dollars and euros and their equivalents in naira, and in case that didn't work, outlines for asylum applications.

'It's only a matter of time,' he would say to Tobe.

So many times, especially when they fought, Tobe wished for that old Harrison. That boy who did not want to ruffle feathers, who wanted, even just for the meantime, to stay hidden with him.

*

Tobe regrets their move to Lagos. If only he had managed Harrison's expectations, if only he hadn't let Harrison set his mind so permanently on something he could not guarantee him. Maybe they would have had a chance. Harrison never liked Lagos and never tried to.

It took him more time than he expected to find his feet, but when he did, he started gathering all his transcripts and recommendation letters and personal statements. He applied to schools in Canada and the UK, Germany and America. After each application, he would wait weeks in crushing uncertainty, irritable and moody. 'They can't refuse all of them,' he said to Tobe. 'One must fall in. Definitely.'

He had been so sure he would get accepted somewhere, and it crushed him when they all accepted him but rejected his scholarship application.

Tobe did not have that problem; he did not need a scholarship. He passed the PLAB 1 test on his first try. When he saw the result, he stared at it for so long, wondering what he was supposed to do with it.

Harrison was elated. 'This is the kind of news I need right now. Progress!' He was laughing. He hugged Tobe tightly, lifting him off the floor till he was standing on the tip of his toes.

'My God,' he continued, and it sounded like his voice was breaking.

'I'm not going,' Tobe said quietly.

'What?'

'I'm not going. I'm not leaving you.'

'What nonsense are you talking? You won't be leaving me. I'll find my way there.'

'I'm not going,' Tobe said again, this time more firmly. A dreadful silence descended.

'You can't be serious,' Harrison said, finally finding his voice.

'I am.'

'But why? Tobe, that test cost two hundred pounds. Two hundred. Pounds!'

There was in Harrison's tone an undercurrent of resentment, as though he held it against Tobe for easily getting this thing they'd both been chasing, only to throw it away. But Tobe was afraid that if he left Harrison, even for a short while, he would not be able to shoulder the crushing weight of Nigeria on his own.

They agreed to wait for Harrison's asylum applications to be approved before moving ahead with PLAB 2. But the asylum applications were worse for Harrison. He knew he had to prove his suffering to unbelieving eyes, but no one warned him of how defeating it would be to go from embassy to embassy trying to convince foreigners that you could no longer survive in your own country, in your own home, that you lived in fear that one day a mob will snatch you off the street and perhaps, no one would hear from you ever again. Still, those applications, too, were rejected. They never spoke about it.

'It's fine,' Harrison would say after getting a rejection. 'Their loss. I had a better chance with the UK anyway.' Or, 'I feel good about Germany after the interview. I'm confident.'

Tobe woke up one night to find him crying. It was after the rejection from Belgium. Harrison was sitting at the edge of the bed, head sunk deep into his palms, bare shoulders shaking. When Tobe placed an arm on his back, his quiet crying turned to heavy sobs.

'What am I supposed to do? Where do they want me to go?'

At Harrison's burial, his mother sat on the ground, her legs stretched out before her, shaking with grief. Once, Adaku came to help her from the ground, but she slumped further down to prevent herself from being picked up.

'Mummy nau,' Adaku said to her mother, exasperated, wiping her own tears with her handkerchief.

They let Tobe sit in the family canopy, a gesture he knew was borne out of guilt. They used to really like him. He used to be at their house all the time, watching Nigerian movies with Harrison's mother or doing Harrison's youngest brother's homework for him while he washed his school uniform. After Harrison told them the extent to which he loved Tobe, the whole family cut both of them off, and while they warmed back up to Harrison over the years, they never spoke to Tobe again.

Sitting there, Tobe did not feel like he belonged with them. But he wanted so desperately to lay claim to Harrison. To assert, even if only with where he sat, that he was family to Harrison. He felt like taking the microphone from the MC and announcing it. He wanted to do something other than feel so helpless and broken. But all he could do was sit there and mourn what could have been if life did not happen the way it did. If it did not take (and take and take) from Harrison till he became a shell of a man, for whom life held no meaning.

After the SSMPA was passed, it was as though a bomb had been dropped on the flat. Tobe would watch Harrison type furiously on his laptop, watch him hiss, watch him trudge from room to room, silent, the crease lines on his brows deepening and deepening. Tobe slowly grew afraid of this consuming anger. An anger he feared might be directed at him just as much as it was directed at President Jonathan. Tobe tried as much as he could to walk around the tension that sat in the flat like charged current. He picked up carelessly flung laundry without mentioning it, stocked the fridge, bought books, tracked down a scarce diffuser they once had that he knew Harrison really loved. He made a show of destroying his party membership card. He would have directly apologized for voting for

Jonathan or for coming from a family ingrained in the Enugu PDP machinery if he knew how.

Lovemaking too became almost a chore, with Harrison talking less and less.

'What's wrong?' Tobe would ask, trying to catch Harrison's gaze.

'Nothing,' would come the reply. 'Nothing. I'm good, why?'

And Tobe had no idea what to do with nothing. After they were spent, Harrison would walk off to watch television or surf the internet leaving him in the chill of their bedroom. Once, Tobe cried, lying there naked on the soft mattress of their bed, the drying beads of sweat still on his body dissipating with the shiver of his tears. Tobe wished Harrison would accuse him of something, lay his blame right in the open so he could at least defend himself.

For the first time since they met, Tobe doubted if Harrison still loved him. Harrison was doing a lot of interviews. Writing Op-Eds in the foreign press. Tobe wanted to say, *Be Careful*, but he feared what Harrison might say in return.

When Harrison started keeping odd hours, Tobe suspected what was going on, but what could he do? He did not have the courage to ask. How would he have even said it? *Are you seeing other men? Are you cheating on me? Are you having an affair? Do you no longer love me?* So he decided he would let it pass.

But then Harrison almost died.

He had gone to meet someone at Oshodi without knowing he was walking into a trap. They wanted his money and his phone, and they threatened to strip him naked and march him through the streets of Lagos if he resisted. Harrison refused to give them his phone or his wallet, refused to remove his clothes. They beat him unconscious.

For days, Tobe sat in his hospital room praying, promising God that if Harrison survived, they would put everything behind them, no questions asked, no grudges held. The possibility of Harrison's death loomed so heavy that when he woke up, Tobe wept with relief.

The first time Tobe saw Harrison's shadow, he thought for a minute that it was him in the flesh and that everything had been one long, cruel dream. Reality was slow to dawn, and when it finally did, it left a heaviness in his chest. As days turned to weeks and weeks turned to months, Tobe lost his grip on Harrison, on the sound of Harrison's voice and what Harrison's beard felt like when he dragged it across Tobe's back.

Many times, Tobe would go to the spot where it happened, and sitting in his car, he would watch the water and cry. Why was their love not enough? Did all these years mean nothing? Seventeen years?

Tobe wanted to know how many people watched and how many people tried to save Harrison. He wanted to go back and care as strongly for the things that mattered to Harrison. Maybe then, somehow, he would have shielded Harrison from this place.

He had thought the worst days were over. During the 2015 election campaign, they knocked on doors for Remi Sonaiya on Sundays, and no matter how worn-out Tobe was, he never complained. It was a sort of reparation for his family's political connections. On the day of the elections, they stood in the long queue and voted for her.

'A real candidate,' Harrison called her. 'Not these paper-cut variations of the same political order.'

She did not win. Buhari swept into power, taking 21 states with him.

Tobe knew she would not win but standing next to Harrison on that day, he had never felt prouder of any vote. Time passed, and as it did, Tobe saw glimpses of the old Harrison return. Maybe in an unguarded smile or in an evening of playing Omawumi on the speaker, in his singing along, in the rhythmic tapping of feet, the gentle movement of his hands. There were times when it really seemed like things were good. Then the news came, seemingly out of nowhere. At first, Tobe thought Harrison had cheated again. And for days after Harrison's death, he berated himself for the anger he felt in those moments, not knowing that all that remained of Harrison was a body.

'I'm so sorry,' Chidi said when Tobe entered the emergency area.

'What happened? Where is he?'

All at once, Tobe wasn't himself, did not know who was on the bed, white as the sheets, in a wet shirt torn straight through the middle and trousers matted to his legs. Or who the surprised nurses were trying to restrain. Tobe only knew that Harrison had died, and for a while, his day had gone on without him knowing.

He returns to that moment, sitting in his car or in his office or at home in Chidi's arms. He returns to the weight of his entire life crumbling. He relives Harrison's day too, or at least the version of it he was able to gather: Harrison's laboured bones carrying themselves to work and going through the choreography of his job and then, with a tired spirit broken too many times in too many places, packing up to leave, mind finally made up. He says goodbye to his colleagues and finds himself here, at this bridge. Tobe likes to think Harrison at least stared at the water for a long time. He likes to think Harrison was conflicted, that their love gave him pause. Tobe imagines that when Harrison climbs the rails, there is shouting, perhaps people running towards him to stop him. Others watch on, bemused, as Harrison takes one last breath. Jumps. And as he struggles for the last time, people line the bridge to look into the water. It brings Tobe some comfort to think that after Harrison jumped, as his life flashed before his eyes, he dwelled, even if for moments, on that room in Parklane, the two of them naked, at ease, safe, the sound of their shared innocent laughter rising and falling, rising and falling.

THE ALIEN NATIVES
Igbẹkẹle Salawu

Sightings of the true picture have been reported in Crimea, Sudan and elsewhere, but this muggy noon when Ben is confronted with the image of dead red colobuses, dead bush rats, and three young poachers in the mangroves of the Niger Delta, he allows himself quick swigs of beer to celebrate the sighting of the truest picture he's ever seen. Forbidden games and children poachers in the backdrop of pandemics suspected to come from those games. He kneels, aims, but the children confound him. Rather than flee like many had done, they take a step forward, and Ben a destabilizing step backwards as if they personify the virus. They sling their kills of monkeys and rats round their bare torsos, contorting their faces and bodies grotesquely as he continues to shift for a better aim.

A woman bounds out like a nursing lioness, sprinting past Ben in seconds, her tresses bobbing against her bum. In a flash, Ben's mind wanders to Julia, to her nimble feet and quick wit. As he readies to shoot, the woman pushes the children off his aim.

Ben swears, then rises, a bottle of beer sliding out of the right pocket of his combat trousers. In less than seven strides, his long legs eat up the distance between them. Towering over them, he holds out his right hand tentatively, then withdraws it abruptly. For another second, his tempest of a mind wonders why he withdrew his hand. Is he fighting the memory of Julia's arm linked with Kofi's, or already afraid of the virus? He is still debating with himself when she breaks the pregnant silence.

'My name is Eva.'

'Efa?'

'Eva! Eva William.'

'Efa Villiam.'

'No, Eva William.'

'I am Ben. Sorry, I don't speak much English.'

Eva flashes her teeth heavenward as she sends peals of laughter to the sky. 'Come and see oyibo that don't speak oyibo!'

Fortuitously for Ben, the quietude of the high noon truncates Eva's attempt at creating a scene. She grasps his hand abruptly, leading the way towards the wicket attached to the fence of the house from which she'd come out to sight the children's kill. 'Oyibo, come, come and see something.'

He allows her to lead him, surrendering to her effervescence, but on second thought, he retracts his hand, becoming embarrassed at being held in public by a buxom woman in a pair of shorts and a decollete top. Or does it again bring the forbidden memory, or is it fear of the virus?

'You from Shell?' Eva asks, recovering from hysteria. 'Oyibo from Shell use to jog reach here, before these militant boys begin kidnap them.'

'No.'

'Chevron?'

'No.'

'Julius Berger?'

'No.'

Eva's vacant stare tells Ben she's run out of multinational companies.

'I am a photojournalist,' he says.

'Wetin that one mean?' Eva asks, her face folding into creases.

'I take pictures for newspapers and—'

'Take my picture,' she interjects, assuming a leaning pose against the fence and making a skewed V-sign with her left hand. 'I want appear in Oyiboland newspaper.' He looks around. 'Where are the boys, and their animals?'

'Wait for me.' She enters the house and reappears with a framed black-and-white picture. Her stubby index finger guides his sight as she orally captions the picture: 'My papa, when he win best student award, his headmaster—oyibo missionary—his papa, his brother, oyibo teacher, another teacher, another oyibo teacher.'

Ben takes in the details of the photograph, from the glad rags of those in it to the mown lawn under their feet, the shipshape hedge behind them and the log cabins in the background. There's pride in Eva's voice as she speaks. 'This is fine picture. Give us picture like this.' She turns around. 'Let me look for my children.'

'No, no.'

She stops, turns back to him.

'I take true pictures.'

'What is "true picture"?'

Ben brushes his dirty blond from quiff to crown. 'Where are they cutting up the animals?'

'They sell them for people selling food.'

'Can you take me there?'

'The food sellers many. I no know who they take it to today.'

'When will your children go again?'

Eva lowers her face as her arms go behind her back, then raises it as her hands relocate to her hips. 'Is it our fault? Yes, we promise say we no go kill the monkeys, but we are hungry.'

'No,' Ben assures, 'it's not about the monkeys.'

Her eyes narrow into a smile. 'Come and see my children when they bathe and dress. Girls *done* already dey chase them. Spirit, the first one, is in senior secondary school. He have three girlfriends already. Action and Government, second and third ones, are in junior secondary. Them done already start to chase girls.'

Ben brushes back his quiff again. 'You need true pictures, Efa; they tell true stories. Then people know, er, what causes diseases; they know the suffering going on here.' He pauses. His speech is still jerky, each phrase rising like a question. All those features that give him away as a non-native speaker of English are still there despite his efforts over the years to suppress them. He inhales deeply and delivers the last statement as declaratively as he can. 'Then rich countries can bring money, a lot of money, to save lives.'

'Ah, money!' Eva chortles. 'Don't worry, I go make it happen this evening. Just give them time to rest.'

'Super!' There's enough beer in the hired car to keep him busy for hours. He has come for true pictures; he will go with true pictures.

'But you must snap me picture first,' Eva demands. 'Me and you together, dressed up.' She guffaws. 'I will put it in Facebook. Me and oyibo in picture. Fine, big men will start looking me.' She breaks into an energetic dance, her arms imitating the motion of paddling a canoe.

'Super!' Ben claps his hands, and Eva's dance becomes more energetic. She yanks off two leaves from the cocoyam plant growing by the fence and starts waving them, one in each hand. But when Ben picks up the small camera resting on his chest, she stops abruptly. 'Go on,' Ben urges, 'it's beautiful.'

'I say "dressed up",' she snaps. 'Which man will look me with this yeye work cloth wey I wear?' She throws the cocoyam leaves away. 'And with oyibo in it, my level done change. Only big big men go come.'

Ben drops the camera; his face also drops, and he dives into the left pocket of his combat trousers.

'You get Facebook account?' Eva asks.

'No.'

Eva cackles with laughter. 'Come and see oyibo who no dey on Facebook.' 'That's for, er, what they call it in English? Privacy, neh?' Ben hands her his business card, which has Ben Müller embossed in gold.

As Ben waits amidst swigs of beer in the hired car that brought him from his hotel room in Yenagoa and will take him back, his satisfaction with Eva's promise is poisoned by her pre-condition. Wouldn't such a picture circulating on social media destroy his prospect of reuniting with Julia?

Two months earlier, Julia had made good on her threat to separate from him after her fourth repetition of the threat. All his marital life, when he was not cities away shooting games or miseries, he was at his desk at home carving his kills before sending them to media houses to dish out. Consequently, Julia had asked him to choose between her and his nomadic occupation. To him then, Julia would never act on the threat to separate from him; he could bribe his way out of such an unthinkable eventuality.

The inaugural bribe was red roses at each return. He would come out of the stadium where he'd shot a game or the scene where he'd shot a misery, and the first thing he'd do was look for red roses. He became a regular customer of the insistent rose hawkers who accosted passersby on the street. But as Julia would not acknowledge the existence of the roses, they would languish untouched. Ben had promptly shopped for another bribe, bringing back exotic art objects from his travels, roaming the antique stores of Hamburg, from Trahbrennbahn Bahrenfeld to Horner Rennbahn, collecting antiques associated with Julia's youth.

The third time Julia told him, in her characteristic declarative tone, 'Quit your job or quit your marriage,' he'd become a denizen of the upmarket stores of Monkebergstrasse, especially Europa Passage, whereupon necklaces and other bling items invaded their flat to take position as peace-making army, where armies of flowers and antiques had been defeated. When again he heard Julia say, 'Your job or me,' he finally awoke into reality, but his tendency to procrastinate situated the danger at an unforeseeable future, luring him to delay conversion from a full-timer to a freelancer till after the following assignment.

When he returned from the assignment to an empty house, he shot after Julia with a volley of calls and texts that must have drained her battery every hour. The calls and the texts, unanswered and unread, made him feel like sewage in a cesspit. He'd underestimated the stabilizing role of Julia on him until then. In the ensuing heart quake, his liver became a casualty as it was lumbered daily with a tsunami of booze. As he spent most of his days sozzled, it became necessary to malinger, enabling him to spend days brooding, swearing after each unanswered call and unacknowledged text. He became retrospectively observant, reliving portentous moments shortly before her departure, moments he hadn't paid attention to. He hadn't seen the red light when she'd stopped pestering him to help around the house, when she'd stopped closing his laptop after he'd ignored her for too long. He'd suspected nothing even when her sonorous voice and animated chats had given way to vocal fries and monosyllables. Rather than alarm, he'd felt relief, deluding himself that she'd finally accepted him the way he was.

In the end, he consulted a shrink, who asked him to stop the calls and the texts. 'She'd separated from you,' he counselled, 'because you haven't been yielding to her requests. By not answering your calls, she's making another request—time to be alone. Not granting that request shows you haven't changed a bit. So your persistent calls are pushing her further away.'

'So I must never call her again?'

'You must wait for the green light from her. And then you mustn't sound desperate.' 'Ah so!' he exclaimed in a fall-rise-fall tune, like a sneeze. 'What about the beer problem?'

'The A. A. to the rescue.'

Outside the Central Station, on his way home, he beheld a sight that scalded his heart as if with molten magma. Julia and Kofi, her immigration client, exchanging glances and smiles, their arms linked. He reeled backwards. Convinced he was swooning, he looked for something to lean on and almost bumped into a junkie resting his back on a wall. He noticed the homeless and the junkies lining the length of Monckebergstrasse from Hauptbahnhof to Rathaus. He saw their serenity. Some of them leaned on trees. Some of them had tins lined up in front of them, each tin labelled with the need to be met with the coins dropped in it. The one he'd almost bumped into had his dog by his side and about ten such tins in his front. Ben read the first three labels: beer, dog, food. He scooped up all the coins in his pockets. 'This never breaks your heart,' he sighed and chucked the coins in the 'dog' tin. He sat beside the junkie, unenthusiastic about going home. He wanted to stay there forever, out of the reach of the nostalgia everything in the house would not stop triggering. He wanted to get his own tins and label them and sit there and drink and never go home again.

Ben opens the wicket, and there is a dead man dolled up in a turtle-necked robe and a top hat in a long ceiling-to-floor banner on the wall of the verandah. He wonders if that is Eva's husband, the father of the three children he'd wanted to photograph. The caption suggests otherwise: 'William Abadi-ingobo, 1930-2000'. The oldest of the children could not be more than fourteen. He wonders why the banner is still there after all these years.

He traces the bleats of goats to an outhouse some yards from the outdoor kitchen. There, an old woman is ringed by about two dozen goats, which she is busy feeding with cassava peels. Though wizened and visibly weak, the critters keep her active.

'Hello,' he shouts. He sees her lips move, but her greeting doesn't make it past the goats' din. Reposed on the wall of the outhouse are three wooden sculptures. He picks up the camera leaning on his chest. The first sculpture depicts a man sitting in a canoe, wearing a turtle-necked robe and a top hat, a rifle in his hand. He pauses. Why rifle? Why not a bow and an arrow? And why the ubiquitous top hats?

The old woman's shout breaks through his thoughts. She's shouting what sounds to him to be somebody's name. Eva appears shortly thereafter from the bungalow that is the main house, her charcoal skin glistening in the subsiding sun. The glorious tresses have disappeared; in their place is a bob cut that is tilted to the left like a hat worn in a hurry. As soon as she takes in the scene, her face crumples into a frown. She strides towards the duo in haste. Her palm reaches out and covers the lens of Ben's camera, which is still pointed towards the sculptures. She lowers the camera back to its idle position on his chest.

'That sounds great,' Ben compliments, referring to the word the old woman had shouted. 'Is that your middle name?'

She grasps Ben's hand abruptly. 'Don't mind that woman,' she says as she drags him away. 'Old age done kill her mind.'

'No, it's beautiful.'

'No, it's my village name.' Her tone has some finality that tells Ben not to pursue that line of discussion further.

When they get to the obituary banner, he asks her, 'Is that your husband, the father of the children?'

'No, my father. The one inside the picture I show you.'

'Ah so!'

'Their fathers be useless men.'

'There are two of them?'

'Three.'

'Ah so! Is that a cultural thing?'

'Which culture? I say they are stupid men. Each of them run away immediately the pregnancy start to dey show.'

Ben sighs in sympathy. 'You must be a strong woman. To have endured three heartbreaks.'

Eva looks sideways at the sated goats that are beginning to scatter in different directions. 'Wetin I go do?'

Ben points at the old woman. 'Is she your mother?'

'No, my grandma.' She points at the close-up in the banner. 'His mother.'

'Are you serious?'

'In her time, many people dey die young, but if you survive, you go live long.'

'And those artworks there, great! I have to get some pictures of them.'

Eva glances over her shoulders. 'Spirit, Action, Government,' she calls her children. 'Oyibo done ready o.'

A waft of fragrance predicts the approach of someone, or some persons. Eva's children file out in order of height: the first one as tall as her, the second at the shoulder of the first, and the third at the shoulder of the second. They come in ironed dress shirts tucked into pleated trousers. Ben glances at his watch.

'Oyibo,' Spirit calls, 'Mama say oyibo is not your language.'

'My language is Deutsch,' Ben intones.

Action dives into his pocket and produces a smartphone. He angles it so that Ben would see it. He steals a sideways glance to see if Ben is impressed. He types 'dush languag' into Google search. 'So you from Netherland?'

'No,' Ben answers, amused. To assuage Action's confused look, he adds, 'Germany.' Confused still, he turns again to his phone, to Google; he types in, reads and looks up. 'But they say Germany speak German.'

Ben enjoys his confusion but is mindful of time. 'Why not go in and get ready first?' The trio run their eyes over their clothing. 'Oyibo, we're ready,' Action says, brushing away imaginary specks of dust from the front of his shirt. 'This one no good?' he asks, indicating his and his brothers' outfits.

'No, it's not good.'

They file back in, appearing again after a few minutes. Their designer polo shirts and jean trousers hug their oiled brown skins. They swagger out as if on a catwalk, their eyes constantly searching Ben's expression for indications of satisfaction.

'Worse,' Ben says.

They file back in. When they return, they have T-shirts on the same jean trousers, and their heads adorned with baseball caps worn askew to show their freshly made short sides haircut.

'Now, this is the worst!'

The children sink to the floor, sitting with their chins on their palms.

'Where are the ones you wore this morning?'

The children gasp. 'Mama say you want show our picture in Oyiboland,' Government says.

'Yes, but you're not looking good for that. They'll think I've taken the pictures in America. They'll think I'm lying.' He looks at Eva, expecting some support, banking on the explanation he gave her a few hours earlier.

Eva shoots him a scowl. 'Why you want make my children look like mad people?'

'Scheize!' he swears. 'I think I explained to you.'

'Yes. And I tell you say I need picture of me and you dressed up. I want put it on Facebook.'

To remain sane, Ben has to remind himself of many things,

of why he is here and what he is doing here. In a flash, they pop into his mind like bullet points in a PowerPoint presentation. It started with Julia's jocular taunt, or taunting joke, delivered in the most orotund voice he'd ever heard her use, the voice he'd always imagined intimidated judges enough to make her win most of the cases she'd handled: 'Why do you go about shooting the afflicted while sparing their affliction?'

They had just enjoyed a full week within which neither had a major assignment. Their tortured marriage had started to heal. Then a call at a dinner table while they were planning a vacation. He was planning to go South to Santorini with Julia; his boss was planning to send him north to Crimea with his camera. Julia had added a rider: 'To think that there's nothing to show for all your overwork.'

Since that day, he's been looking for an opportunity to prove Julia wrong. Then three things happened at the same time, and he's in the Niger Delta. First, there was an urgent need for an endangered species advocacy concerning some primates in the Niger Delta, most especially the red colobus, which had been eaten almost to extinction and whose staple shrub was also roasting away in the oil that kept spilling and being spilt. Then there were outbreaks of viral epidemics in Africa and Asia which were traced to the eating of some animals, among them monkeys and rats, the more reason why there had to be advocacy to stop the eating of the Niger Delta red colobus. When things couldn't get worse, Julia separated from him. When Kofi came into the picture, he found himself burdened with the need to prove wrong not only Julia's words but also her choice. Also, he had to go as far from home as possible to alleviate the pain. So he found it easy to convince his editor he could contribute to nature advocacy and help halt the advance of the viruses by creating awareness about unsafe culinary cultures through photojournalism.

Most of the viruses had no cure yet, but he steeled himself, asking what better opportunity there was to cut the picture of a hero than to descend right into the hellhole and come out with pictures of horror with which to shame Julia's choice and probably win a Pulitzer prize to be dedicated to her as an irresistible bribe. Besides, wasn't the epidemic still in Congo and two neighbouring countries, thousands of kilometres from Nigeria, which wouldn't reduce the heroism as Africa was one? Wasn't Julia's separation worse than the African virus?

Now, the certainty is gone; every hour edges him closer to regret. He felt no disappointment at the airport in Port Harcourt; after all, nobody would expect an airport to be constructed out of raffia. But the closer he got to his destination, the farther from it he felt. Dugouts paddled on creeks were all he was shown throughout the ride as native culture as if hundreds of boats were not to be found on the canals of the Elbe.

Now in his rural destination, everywhere he looks, the women are in shorts or minis and the men in jeans. Everybody is Angella or Goodluck, Blood (of Jesus) or Manager. The most semblance of Africa he's seen were hunters with dead games dripping blood on their bare bellies. It is disappointing enough that they were all toting guns—no bows and arrows—but it is disastrous that they invariably apologized for the slight trace of pristine Africanness by fleeing or being pushed off the gaze of his camera. He is unsure whom they thought he represented: the persuasive conservationists they had promised—and now fail—or the government-employed, matter-of-fact epidemiologists—to whom they had shown many centenarians who had eaten monkeys and rats from infancy.

'Clap-clap,' Eva's claps drill into Ben's protracted horizon-gazing reverie. His scrunched face looks around as if making sense of a strange planet.

'Oyibo!' Eva calls in a voice that expresses growing horror.

Ben casts his gaze towards his interlocutors. 'Where is Africa?'

Answer comes in four death stares directed at him.

'Where is Africa?' Ben asks again, looking from the increasingly horrified mother to the now sniggering children.

Eva raises her right index finger. All redirect their gaze towards her. Facing her children, she raises the index finger to the right side of her head, above her ear. She taps at the same spot three times. The sniggers on the faces of the children morph instantly into epiphany. They cast Ben a gaze of intense pity.

'Show me Africa,' Ben says, 'and I'll shoot you.'

The children exchange puzzled glances, epiphany overtaken by bewilderment. With a single leap, the closest among them to the door hightails it indoors, followed by the second— with two leaps—and the third—with three leaps. Eva looks from Ben to the fleeing children, torn between fear and confusion. Spirit pops out. 'Mommy, he is not oyibo.' He grabs his mother by the hand and pulls her indoors.

Ben sees the door slammed and hears it bolted from behind. He can still hear them from behind the door.

'See his name inside the card he give you. Ben. Like Bin Laden.'

'See that surname too. Who be Mullah? Not those Muslims from the North?' 'You done ever see oyibo that don't speak oyibo?'

'You done ever see oyibo dey roam inside bush?'

'He be one of those light-skin Fulani. Some of them be cattle herdsmen, some of them be beggars.'

'Maybe this one run mad, he come lost inside forest.'

'Maybe he no run mad. Maybe them send am to come pretend like he be oyibo so that them go know how them go attack us.'

'Yes o. See many many places them done attack.'

'The next thing, he want shoot us.'

'Thank you Lord for this revelation. Them done discover another tactic to spy us. We must warn our people.'

Ben teeters to his hired car. The chauffeur lies half spread-eagle on the back seat, dead to the world. Ben taps his leg, and his arms respond, lifting up his torso. When he taps his leg again, the scaffold of his arms collapses, and he returns to his former posture. He then slaps his leg, and the driver rises with a start, spins round and squints his way back into the world. He fumbles in his shirt and trouser pockets for the car key, casts vacant glances about like a person dizzied by a blow to the head. Then he catches sight of Ben and stabilizes. 'Oga,' he hails, using the honorific for superiors.

'Where is Africa?'

The chauffeur's face puckers up. 'Oga?' he calls with a rising tone as if he's unsure if it's still Ben. The chauffeur raises his right index finger to the right side of his head, above his ear. He taps at the same spot three times. 'Oga?' He taps three times again, then shakes his head in pity.

During the ride back to his hotel in Yenagoa, Ben keeps looking left and right, asking, 'Where is Africa?' —being answered by the twitters of birds on the trees flying by, the images of young people in ripped blue jeans, the latest models of Mercedes Benz, Toyota, Honda, BMW and Volkswagen speeding by.

SMALL HOUSING
Tafadzwa Z. Taruvinga

After Tommy comes a Bleck Zimbabwen
Sandra

'Ouch! Too hot, too hot, too hot.'

Mntsm, I keep forgetting to switch off the geyser. With Sam not yet paying my bills, I need to be more vigilant.

There . . . that's much better.

Oops, be careful, Sandy. Falling in this tub will break your old back. Yes, if you're twenty-four and unmarried in 1996, you, my friend, are ageing. If you weren't, why else would Tom have let you go? Face it, he has probably found someone younger and more exciting. Or he has always had someone you didn't know about.

That time he took me to London and left me at the hotel, I should have insisted on going with him to meet his so-called sister. I was so pissed off, but I forgave him after he ordered room service and made sweethoney love to me the next morning. Maybe I was in denial. What if he had gone off to a wife or girlfriend? Tommy had his secrets that I never asked about, but I knew they existed. I was the fool, not wanting to accept that I was nothing to him more than an occasional good time.

A sister in Birmingham that I had never heard of? He went there at least four times a year. I should have put two and two together. What an idiot, Sandy. For a smart girl, what a fool you are. You gave the man everything, and he couldn't even take you anywhere besides bloody Joj Hotel. What's Avondale when a man can take you to Birmingham? Fine, he flew you to London that one time, but you know very well that Joj is a hideout for married men and their small houses.

'It's Ge-ooor-ge,' Tommy would say whenever he thought I had pronounced the word wrong—but it's my playful Shonglish that I sometimes choose to speak—as if I didn't go to a school where the English teacher was English. As if I didn't get an A for both language and literature at O level. I often told him that I got four As and two Bs, plus I passed my A levels with ease.

'Still, it's Ge-ooor-ge,' he'd say.

'It's Joj, iwe Thomas. I'm not a mukiwa like you, I'm a Bleck Zimbabwen, and you just have to deal with that. Besides, you understand what I'm saying. And more importantly, you love me with my Shonglish and my flaws, no?'

'Your flaws, you say?'

'Yes, my Shonglish flaws. Shut up and kiss me.'

We always closed our eyes when we smooched. And we did so anywhere we wanted. We didn't care about the staring eyes around us. Zimbabweans are not comfortable with people who show affection in public. But that didn't matter to me. I felt free to be myself when I was with Tom.

'I do love you, Sandy-randy,' he often said while embracing me.

'Let's go to Joj, my love, kwaJojo,' I'd say.

I'd have done anything for Tom. They should call that place Joj Broth-tel. And I'd be the escort, won't I? The prostitute who paid her customer in kind over two wasted years. Yes, I'm the stupid one who settled Tom's bill with my heart. Oh Tommy. You're such a cow. A big cowardpig, Tommy you. I nlove and miss you so much, my darling. Oh, stop it, foolish woman! This is exactly why Pelagia hands you over to the barman and leaves. 'Any little memory and your Kariba floodgates burst open. Haargh, I'm tired of your whining like a mosquito, and I'm going,' she says.

Shower, please wash away these tears. Make them not count, forever. Welcome to the real world, Sandy. Tommy is gone. Tommy is gone for good, woman. What did you imagine, though? That the guy was going to marry you—some Bleck, township girl—and do what? Take you to Britain to live in *The Bodyguard* with him like Rachel Marron and Frank Farmer? Are you a dolt?

But you know what? I'm smart, and I've worked my way across town to Avondale. You'll come out of this, Sandybabe. Besides, Tommy is just a farm boy from Marondera who has had enough of the natives and wants to go back to being British again. My very own mukiwa. Though he never told me why he left, I can't imagine he'd opt for a white woman just because he's white, no. He loved that we were different. Plus, he always complimented my intelligence that complemented his. And he loved this song, oh Lord, he loved 'Daisy'. Too bad I can't run to the radio to turn up the volume, but this part reminds me of when he sang it—

Are you feeling alri—ght, bay—bay?

He loved this track, but he couldn't dance at all, not even for a rabbit five-cent coin. Tom danced like he had used condoms for legs. I thought it was amusing when he did. You're so handsome. That person in London who took away my nTommy is one lucky girl. My husband and the father of my babies that never was. Shame, Sandra. He once said one day we would make our own little 'Andy Brown' and, as soon as he could talk, we would make him sing *Daisy* better than *this* Andy Brown. I remember how hard we laughed when he said that. I had hoped to get pregnant since I had secretly taken myself off the pill. He would have married me then. I'm sure he would have.

Anyway, to hell with Tommy. I will find another mukiwa to marry me. Hell will freeze over before I marry a Shona man. They irritate me with their rules and traditions. Do this, don't do that, drink this, don't drink that. Ah, who needs those puppet strings from the iron age? I love my *Jameson,* and Tommy did too. Gosh, the sex we did after having a few glasses was out of this world. He drove me crazy with his wet big shiny redhead. We called it that. Anyone who says white men have a small one needs to see-saw on Tommy's bazooka, haha-da! That would change their minds.

Stop it! Stop thinking about zexual indakoss. (Pelagia's imagination amazes me.) It's too early to give Sam your chocolata, especially before your heart has healed. It's only been a year since Tommy left you. Hmmm, yes . . . that's why you've just shaved your chocolata and legs, Jezebel. You think you're so clever. Quit that fake innocent look; it suits you only a little. You know exactly what you're doing. Stop looking at me before I break this mirror in your face, slart. That's what Pelagia would call you if she were here.

You have no shame, you who dares wipe the steam off this mirror so you can see your face better. The man has taken you out for a meal five times in four months, and you're ready to bed him? Well, he seems like a gentleman, maybe a little more adventurous and a little less stuck up than the average Shona man. He's a bit of a Tommy, isn't he? Letting you drink your whisky if you want to and everything else that sets you free. Breaking all the rules. Giving you space and time for you to get comfortable first before letting him into your—

Orgh, this whisky is just right with two blocks of ice.

Cocoa butter for my body, check; Pond's for my cheeks, check; Ingram's Camphor Cream for my feet, check; a splash of Fa in my armpits, doesn't stain my bras and blouses, check; olive oil for my straightened Afro, check; a little of the Revlon rose lipstick that

Tommy bought me in London that isn't too suggestive, check.

Besides my red nail polish that needs a touch-up, but not today, I'm done with my scrubbing, oiling, spraying and blowing reechwol by the second hour since getting home at 3 p.m. On Fridays, Mr Mubayiwa leaves the office at 11:30 for a midday tee-off at Chapman Golf Club. Once I'm done tidying up the week's work, he said, I can leave at any time after two, but only on Fridays. On the other four days, I work until five, with a forty-five-minute lunch break, instead of the one hour that the rest of the back-office staff take. I enjoy working at Founders Bank's CBD branch, and Mr Mubaiwa is very professional.

I've told Bhigi at the gate that I'm expecting Samuel around half past five. Bhigi is overprotective and maybe even a little jealous of any other man spending time with me. Come to think of it, he never got along with Tommy. So, I had to tell him in advance that Sam was coming over for the first time and that he should be nice. Anyway, let's see how things go with Sam. I don't want to excite myself for a Shona man who might disappoint me after all. But the few occasions we have spent time together, he has been a real gem-gem. Sam the gem-tall-man, haha-da.

My lunch break is short, but last time he made sure we met and ate quickly before we both had to go back to work. He had already ordered my favourite meal at Maguta Café in Eastgate: brown sadza, peanut-buttered muboora, and a tasty roadrunner stew with chilli. Yummy. The other times we met were over early dinner at different spots around town. At least Sam doesn't take me to Joj Hotel like Tommy. He always eats light so that he can eat some more when he gets home to his wife.

Sam and I met in the most interesting way at a phone booth on First Street. I was foraging for some coins in my handbag. People behind me in the queue started complaining, telling me to step aside and give the next person a chance if I didn't have money to make a call. As if out of the blue, Sam walked towards me and handed me three one-dollar coins. He then walked away without saying anything other than, 'Go on, make your call. I know we'll meet again.'

He was clean-shaven, dressed to the tee in a grey suit, white shirt and blue tie, and he smelled edible. Who among those queuing complainers would dare to ask this Johanthan-Denga-of-a-man anything about him delaying my making a call? Sam vanished into First Street's lunchtime bustle. I called my crazy brother and his stupid wife again and gave them a piece of my mind for disrespecting Amai the way they had. I can never make a call like that from the office. I don't want people there to know my business.

I didn't see Sam again for maybe two weeks until one time, just after I had crossed Samora Machel, walking towards Julius Nyerere. There, near the National Gallery's entrance, I'd usually find a Rixi Taxi to take me home after work.

'Excuse me,' said Sam, and I turned around.

He didn't want to show me that he had noticed how surprised I was to see him again.

'Yes?' I said.

'I have another three dollars in my pocket, and I was wondering if you would like to help me spend it on some drinks somewhere nearby,' he said. That was smooth, my goodness. Sam is very good with words. I didn't show him that he impressed me. I just laughed.

'Oh, it's you again.'

'Yes. Did I not say I would see you again?'

'I guess you did. So, do you always walk around with three dollars in your pocket to give someone? Anyone?'

'Until one meets a woman like you, he could never fathom the true value of a few silver coins.'

'You,' I said, unable to control my giggle and unsure if I could counter his charm.

'I see you want to get home before it gets dark. May I have your telephone number? That way I can ring you at a more convenient time, you see?'

'Uhm . . .'

I was speechless.

'Is that a yes?' asked Sam

'No, I'm sorry. I must go home, but maybe next time. Good seeing you anyway.'

'Not a problem, madam. But where and how do I find you?'

'I can't give you my work telephone number, and I don't have a line at home.'

'Then at least tell me where you work. I would like to bring you lunch soon.'

'Hmmm, maybe next time,' I said.

'Alright, that's okay. Can I at least have your name?'

'It's . . . Sandra,' I said, hoping he hadn't noticed my hesitation.

'Okay, Sandra. I'm Samuel, but you can call me Sam. It's nice to meet you,' he said, offering his hand.

I shook it only with my fingers. Ah! A lady must pretend to be shy for a while to see how persistent a man is.

'Same here,' I said.

'Go on. I will see you around, Sandra,' he said before we each walked away.

I did not turn around, but I knew he had. I could feel it. I was feeling him too, though I had noticed the wedding ring on his finger. Anyway, I knew I would meet him again because Harare is tiny. And I can spot a well-groomed man from a mile. As fate would have it, we bumped into each other again a few weeks later at a small seminar that the Reserve Bank was hosting for banks, accounting firms, and insurance houses.

Then, I failed to escape and gave Sam my work number. He's like a leopard preying on a gazelle: patient but persistent. In the weeks that followed, he phoned me at work. We spent time together when it was possible. He never pretended not to be married with four kids. I should have walked away, but there's something about Sam that I can't resist, Shona though he is. I can't quite place my finger on it. It's probably his gentle nature that gets me. I might have just found my Blek Tommy. My Sammy—

Slow down, sister.

Two soft knocks on my door wake me from my daydreaming. Since I got home, I've drunk three double whiskies without realising it. Andy Brown has since stopped playing. Maybe it's time for Sammy's music now. He said he goes for something like Simply Red or Marvin Gaye, but I won't play *Sexual Healing*. Then why the naughty giggle, Sandy?

'Comiiing,' I yell while quickly changing the cassette and pressing PLAY on *Marvin Gaye's Greatest Hits*—the one with *Mercy Mercy Me* on it. Oh no! The first song on that album is *Let's Get It On*. Sandy, you are. Just. So. Bad.

I can't believe Sam is standing on the other side of this door. Pelagia's words keep going around in my head: 'The best way to get over a man who has broken your heart is to get under a new one. Hydrate him, but don't give your heart so quick.'

She was chewing some potato crisps with her mouth open when she said that. Like a slart. I haven't told her about Sam, by the way. I can just hear her saying, 'Yes, I said a new man, sister girl, but I never said a married one!'

What are you doing, Sandra? You, the small house of a married man? Well, a nice married man.

Check your hair first. Not in the bathroom mirror, you gizzard. You have a wall mirror in this lounge. Okay, the hair looks fine. You haven't smudged your lipstick . . . yet. Another sip of whisky, yes! Now you're ready to meet the man. Go!

'Hello, Sam.'

'Hi Sandra. These are for you.'

'Oh my, you didn't have to, but thank you very much. These are beautiful.'

'And this too.'

'Wait a minute now. Sam, are you trying to get me drunk?'

'Drunk? Oh no, never. Not me. Maybe a teeny-tiny tipsy, I will admit,' he says. We laugh.

'Come in, come in.'

Sam towers into the room, and I close the horny devil's creaking door behind a married saint.

Conquering a small island
Samuel

Slow down, Sam. Natal Road is around the corner, and Sandra is not going anywhere. Besides, you are to court her for a while, meaning you may not bed her today. Do you not want to keep this woman for some time, not because Amai has insisted on wanting a boy grandchild, but for your sake?

'You want me to die a slow death, Sameri. To leave this earth having only seen your female offspring is wasting me away to the winds of Gutu village. We need a son. Don't you hear the whispers of this land that are traded at the river? Quiet yourself and listen. They say my son cannot birth a son,' said Amai a while ago.

Have you not secretly heeded the advice of Isaac and Phineas, even though they blurt a thousand nonsensical things when the fumes of their zambezis have drowned the pistons of their minds?

'A woman on the side is a catalyst for your marriage, pal. We have been at it for years, and our wives are m-m-much happier than before. Actually, it's, it's a perfect serup, Mr Bvute. Each time you get home after leaving your s-ssside woman, it feels like your wife has been, has been rebranded. Think about it, Sammy boy, think about it, maaaan,' they say while I pretend to ignore them.

'You are both drunk. Your ideas are wild,' I say.

Maybe you have been listening to them and Amai, and now you are here, Sam. A discreet woman like Sandy could be a lubricant to this marriage. But you must be one hundred and twenty per cent sure that Betty never finds out, or this would devastate her. You do not want to hurt your wife, Sam. She has already been through enough.

I arrive at the flower shop in no time.

'Hello, Sam. The most romantic husband in Harare. I knew it was you the second that bell tinkled fervently like it always does when you visit us. It's nice to see you again, dear. Mwah, mwah.'

'Rosie, keeper of all of Zimbabwe's beautiful flowers. It is good to see you.'

'Oh, stop it, you cunning devil. That's why Betty will never leave you.'

'I am the lucky one, my dear.'

'That you are, Sam. That you are. So, what are you getting for Betty today?'

'I will go with the usual, I think. She loves that bouquet that you do so well.'

'Coming right up! Tsitsi, will you bring me a bunch of D63s from the cold room, please dear?'

'Yes, ma'am, right away.'

'Maybe some chocolates and a bottle of a Mukuyu red to go with that, Sam?'

'Perhaps a box of Rochers, actually. Thank you, Rosie. That will do for today. I must keep some of that romance in store for the years to come, you know.'

'Oh Sam, you just won't stop.'

'Come in, come in,' says Sandy.

'What a lovely place you have here.'

'Thank you. Can I take your jacket?'

'Yes, of course, thank you.'

'Please, take a seat. Anywhere you like.'

She pours a double for me.

'Some ice, Sam?'

'Yes, please, thank you.'

Shit, the condoms. I left the condoms in the car. With AIDS these days, one can never take chances, beautiful though a woman might be and tempting as nyoro is.

'Raw is delicious, guys, but wrapping your sweet in the paper is better,' says Eazy. Pheeny always begs to differ and vows his loyalty to nyoro even though he dips his straw in several bittersweet cocktails around town. One day mukondombera will kill him and his wife, we often warn him.

'Sandy darling, I should check if I closed my windows properly. Will be right back.'

'Darling you say. Is this your way of asking me out, Sam?'

'Hold that thought. I will be right back.'

'Okay, I will put the flowers in the vase so long.'

I hasten myself down the stairs and into the dashboard, shoot a glance at the gatekeeper—Sandra says everyone calls him Biggy— and run up the stairs. I pause to catch my breath before entering Sandy's flat again.

'Is everything okay?'

'Yes, oh yes.'

'Sorry, but I didn't cook, Sam. I'm usually not this lazy, but this week has been hellish. I can always go and order something from Moyo's if you're hungry.'

'No, no, Sandy, relax. I thought we could just talk and enjoy a drink. Come and sit here with me. You are so far away in that kitchen.'

'Okay. Here I come. I'm done with, with the nflowers.'

Sandra catwalks towards me with her usual confidence.

'Cheers, Sam,' she says before she sits on the other sofa.

'Cheers, Sandy darling.'

'Oh, a loud clink. That seems to suggest a toast. May I ask you to toast for us? Besides—about this 'darling' thing—you had something to say when you ran downstairs.'

'Oh yes, I remember.'

'Tell me then, Sam.'

'Instead of toasting, there is something important I would like to say. But I cannot compete with the great Marvin Gaye singing *Mercy Mercy Me*, and you know that. So, I think you should come closer, and I will tell you what's on my mind.'

'Alright, Sam, I will move just a little up to . . . say, here.'

'A little more?'

'Mkay, to . . . here?'

'A liiittle more . . .'

'Ah Sam, you're sneaky. Can I trust you?'

Oh, mercy, mercy me, I am about to embarrass myself with this stalagmite. Crossed legs might rescue you, sir. Cross your legs, presto.

'Oops, careful now. Do not fall and hurt yourself, love. Where are you going?'

'I want to get you a coaster. What you want to tell me, mbetter be good, Mister Ss-ssaaam.'

When Sandra staggers back with a coaster in hand, I tell her that since I met her four months ago, I have not stopped thinking about her. I thank her for the times we have met to have lunch and for inviting me to her flat. She asks me what makes me different from other men who break hearts at will, and I promise her that I am a man of my word, that I would never break her heart if she gave me a chance to love her. Besides, would I have told her that I am married if I were dishonest? And does such honesty not prove good intention? She asks if I think ill of her for seeing a married man, and I return an emphatic, 'No, no, no, not at all, darling. You are following your heart in the same way that I am.'

In the words of Eric Clapton, Sandra looks wonderful tonight. Losing herself to me and her sincerity instantly accentuate her beauty and this damn thing. For the first time in years, because I make love to Betty every other month when she perhaps feels guilty for turning away from my caresses, I feel alive and wanted. That Sandra is young and impassioned is exhilarating.

'Do . . . do you have mfeelings for me, Sam?'

'Oh yes, my darling. I would not be here if I did not. I want you to be with me and for you to show me what it feels like to be young agai—'

'So nthis is what you're after? Excitement and the adventure that is warming yourself between a younger woman's thighs?'

'Yes . . .'

'Ah! What nonsense, Sam!' she says, laughing, slapping my arm and drawing closer to me.'

'You did not let me finish, Sandy.'

'I will, but first your proposition.'

'Okay. This is what I think. Do you own this place, hmm?'

'That is your . . . p-proposition?'

'Hear me out, my lady. Well, do you?'

'No, I'm renting it.'

'So let me buy it for you, simple.'

'Sam, we've known each other for only four months. That is a huge commitment.'

'Four months in which I have fallen in love with you.'

'Oh, do you nreally mean that, Sam?' she asks, tears welling up in her eyes.

'I do, and I will prove it. Let me buy this place for you, and we can make a home of it. What sayest you?'

Sandra urgently plugs her lips onto mine, forgetting about the glass in her hand. I do not think she minds its contents splashing onto her new beige rug. The breathing between us could fog up the mirror hanging on the wall. Marvin Gaye breaks into a *Distant Lover* wail that sends us into a whirlwind. We are hardly as distant as he suggests, although, in another sense, we also are. The escapade that is Sandra promises to be magical. Her kisses, like a dream come true, are just what I imagined: hard, heartfelt and laden with lust. She straddles me to reveal a pair of silky thighs hidden beneath her light dress.

'Oh my, you're quite the man, Sam.'

'Well—'

'Shut up and kiss me, Sam. Here. Touch me here,' she says, planting my palm on her chest.

Marvin Gaye stops singing, except he does not, drowned by Sandra's heavy breathing. I lift myself up in a quick manoeuvre that places petite Sandra's legs around my waist and her arms around my neck. We zig-zag across the room, ignoring the fallen side table, past a standing lamp next to a door leading into a passage that leads to her bedroom.

There, Sandra hurriedly unbundles my belt buckle, the button beneath it, then my shirt-n-tie. She accelerates my slouching trousers onto the floor with her feet; I loosen the shoulder-clutching strings of her dress; she bites my lip and sucks my tongue; I ditto; we smile into each other's eyes; I undo the clips of her brassiere, getting drunk on the scent of her hair; she tells me to take off her lace panties as if she contravened the law and deserves punishment (her words not mine) and asks me to suck her breasts. My tongue wets her nipples as though her breasts might suffocate me into a death that the police and Betty would fail to comprehend; my fingers are everywhere on and in her; she feasts on my stalagmite, completely gives herself to me and asks me to make love to her. She says she loves me and calls me Big Sammy. I must gnash my teeth to avert anything premature. I decidedly run through my mind anything other than Sandra's—

Other things, other things, other things, other things. Inflation rate; income statement; annual financial statements; provision for bad debts; cars, yes, the new Nissan Hardbody, oh no, that will not work, the Toyota Corolla maybe; South Korea; Ouagadougou; carburettor; Mugabe's Economic Structural Adjustment Programme, ESAP, ESAP, ESAP, ESAP—

'Gosh, yes, Nsammy, yeeesss!'

Please stop moaning like that, woman.

'Is that a yes to my proposal, Sandy babe?'

We laugh in-between little but storming raptures. She shrieks as if for her neighbours and Biggy at the gate to hear. If he does, then good. Sandy is now Big Sammy's woman, sorry, small Biggy. You lose.

'Oh, gggg-gah! Amaihwe-e, Sam!'

'Is *this* good?'

'Shit, you make love to me like you're conquering a small island, Ns-aaa-mmmy! Whose son are you?'

By the time we descend onto her big pillows at the end of it all, a pair of Jamaican hundred-metre-sprinters could not have perspired more.

'Lord, I'm thirsty. Please, may you get me some water, Big Sammy?'

I head out through the passage to the kitchen past the lounge.

'And some more whisky, please.'

Heading back, I notice the rest of the furniture in the lounge for the first time. The place is neat and understated but comfortable. Two long cream sofas that are perpendicular to each other, a small glass-top coffee table in the middle that has been skewed by the violence of eager loins, a display cabinet standing against the wall opposite the one with the big mirror, several Hottentot artworks, a television and a radio, each in a wooden cabinet that is next to the door through which I earlier scurried downstairs for condoms.

'Are you ready to go again after this round of whisssky?' asks Sandy, so we do for half an hour more. After, when Sandy doses off, I slide out of bed to take a shower. She mumbles a spent, 'Do you want me to come and help you find some towels?'

'No, I will be okay, my darling. Get some rest.'

I dress up after a quick shower, and I am sure to lightly apply the Vaseline petroleum jelly that I have found in her cabinet. Any fragranced lotion will be unfamiliar to Betty. I wake up Sandy to kiss her goodbye promising to phone her on Monday morning at work.

'Do you want me to walk you out, mbaby?'

'No, my darling. Stay in bed. Does the door lock itself after I close it so that you are safe?'

'Yes, baby. You're sweet, Nsammy.'

'I will see you soon, pretty lady. I must go now.'

As I lift the small table that fell onto the lounge's wooden floor and the whisky glass off the rug, I hear Marvin bidding his audience farewell at the end of *My Love is Waiting* live in concert. It feels, instead, like twenty thousand fans are applauding my conquest of a young, delectable woman who has stolen my heart, my darling small house. You still have what it takes, old man, conqueror of small islands.

I seldom arrive home beyond seven, so I must think of a good excuse for Betty.

ELEVATOR JOHNSON
Uchechi Princewill Akachi

Elevator Johnson, in boxer shorts, leaned over the low rail on the balcony of his apartment on the 232nd floor and flashed his barcoded forearm at the idling drone watching from just inside the troposphere over Century Plaza, Owerri. He could not see it, only those on the 400th floor had ever claimed to glimpse the thing, but the green luminescence that flashed over his barcode signalled that it saw him, and that was all that mattered. It would send him his taxi.

He walked back into the apartment, making sure to fasten the latch on the balcony entrance behind him, and started to throw his clothes back on. The compound display on his wall-to-wall digiset was full of the news. All seventeen streams he could afford greeted him with the same boring image of an ethnically generic man and woman in grey or black or blue suits discussing the same breaking news: aliens. Which was a shame because he had wanted to see Caillou.

The elevator ride down to the ground floor was uneventful, and Johnson found his taxi waiting for him the moment he left the building.

'Elevator Johnson Mbadiwe?' The hip twenty-something driver

called out. Three of his teeth were gold, and he wore a heavy cross around his neck.

'Yes. That's me.'

'Cool. Mind if I get confirmation from above?' The driver thrust his arm out the window, exposing his barcode. Johnson flashed his forearm at the sky, and both their arms lit up simultaneously.

'Sweet,' the driver grinned, 'God approves.'

Johnson snorted and got into the backseat.

'What?' The driver asked with an even bigger smile. 'You don't believe in the big guy?'

Johnson provided an apologetic smile.

'Oh, I understand. It's okay, man. The big guy reaches us all differently. Besides,' the driver laughed, 'God may not exist. But aliens sure do.'

On the mile-high billboards floating above the streets of Owerri, one video clip played over and over again, punctuated by broadcast after broadcast of news anchors debating famous scientists. It showed alien ships, with technology that managed to outstrip Earth's in every way possible, barreling through the inner Van Allen belt in a tight spiralling orbit, unravelling dozens of artificial gravitomagnetic defences like peeling an orange.

Fifteen minutes later, Johnson stepped out of the taxi and into the Horizon Beta Home Complex. Though not as luxurious as Horizon Alpha, the individual monoliths that assaulted his vision still stank of old money. Money made from mining superdense iron from the core used in the production of the first and most stable gravitomag engines. Or perhaps even older money than that, money from oil.

Real gravel crunched under his thick rubber boots as he made his way to Beta 109 and rang the bell. The front door of Beta 109 doubled as a floor-to-ceiling two-way digiset with sixty-nine streams. If he hadn't already seen it this morning, he'd have gawked and sputtered. Instead, he tsked. If Johnson bought subscriptions to sixty-nine streams, he wouldn't have an apartment to watch them in. There was nothing quite as depressing as rich people so casually reminding you of the gap between you.

It didn't take long before all sixty-nine streams blinked out and were replaced by a face. With an eyebrow raised and lips pursed, the face regarded Johnson with mild interest.

'Good afternoon, Mrs Belsinth.' Johnson nodded at the image on the display.

The face blinked at him. 'You're the elevator guy.'

'Elevator Johnson, ma'am.'

'Yes. Silly name. You've fixed my elevators this morning. And they work.' She said, then disappeared for a moment. Through the in-display speakers, Johnson could hear the faint ping of elevator doors opening and closing, and then the face came back. 'And they still work now. There's nothing wrong with them.'

'Yes, ma'am. Your elevators are fine.'

She nodded, pleased, then narrowed her eyes at him. 'So, why are you here, Elevator Man?'

'Elevator Johnson, ma'am. Sorry to bother you, but I'm here because I left something behind. A textbook I had with me when I came this morning. *On the Mechanics of Ninth Through Eleventh Generation Gyroelectrically Stable Elevators* by Trisha Kingsley. I think I left it on the oak table in the family room.'

There was a brief pause, and then, 'Give me a moment.'

The ping of the elevators came through the speakers again, and the display switched back to showing sixty-nine streams.

Johnson tsked, folding his arms against his chest. The lady, Mrs Belsinth, felt like one of those people. She would think he had forgotten his book on purpose just so he could be in her house again, and she wouldn't say anything to him, but his referrals in Horizon Beta would begin to drop as the housewives gossiped. He regretted bringing the book with him. He had been far too anxious about the high-level coils in the gyro-stable models. He hadn't needed the book anyway. It had only been a wiring issue.

Conversation filtered from the streams into Johnson's ears. A bleak-looking news anchor on one stream interrogated a dark-haired bespectacled scientist.

'Dr Okorafor. Your people in the space agencies never fail to remind us that we have our own spacefaring technology, and only bureaucracy has kept us from exploring beyond our solar system. Why is it that, with all our advances, our scientists cannot recognize any of the technology used by the aliens in this invasion? Are they that much better than us?'

'Well, Frank, the thing is we're looking at a completely different civilization.'

'Uh huh. Go on, doctor.'

'The working theory is not that they are that much more advanced. In fact, we think they're only slightly so. We recognize many of the things their technology is doing. It's just that they are doing it differently from us, with the same or slightly better results.'

'I find that very hard to believe.'

'Parallel evolution, Frank. We advanced alongside our discovery of gravitomagnetic technology. They seem to have developed along something else. Another direction, so to speak. A direction that we have very little experience in.'

'Dr Okorafor, ma'am, the experts on the internet forums are calling your theory bullshit. Isn't this just a polite way of saying we can't stop them?'

The voices from the TV cut off sharply as every one of the sixty-nine streams switched to the same live news update. In the footage, alien ships descended from black space into blue sky. Each one was an elongated oval of blinding chrome nestled inside a dark metal spiral coiled along its long axis. To Johnson, they resembled shiny metal eggs set inside black springlike cocoons moulded to their frame. The news update sat stiff across the footage in block letters, a grim voiceover reading the words for good measure. The aliens had just exited low orbit at high speed and entered the upper ionosphere. Extraterrestrials were now less than 500 kilometres away from Earth's surface.

The news blinked away, and Mrs Belsinth's irritated face reappeared in the door's display.

'There are so many books on that table. I keep telling the kids that the family room is no place for their books, but Hyacinth sets such a bad example, and when a father keeps doing something, the children stop listening to their mother when she complains about it.'

'Yes, ma'am, I'm sorry, but my book is specifically, *On the Mechanics of Ninth Through Eleventh Generation*—'

'Oh, I know. It's there. Terribly heavy thing. Hardcover.'

'Yes, ma'am.' Johnson sighed with relief.

'Well, don't just stand there. Come in and get it.'

'Alright, ma'am,' Then after a pause, 'if you would open the door.'

'Oh. Of course. Put your barcode up against the display. I need to verify your identity. I mean, I recognize you, but have you seen the news today? Aliens, of all things. I mean, you could be one.'

'They haven't gotten here yet.' Johnson stifled an eye roll and pressed his forearm against the display. 'And I doubt very much that they look anything like us.'

'Well, we can't be too careful, can we?' Mrs Belsinth clucked. 'Verified. You can come in now.'

The door slid open, and Johnson walked in the mansion to find Mrs Belsinth walking out of an elevator to meet him.

'I'm not lifting that thing. Is fixing elevators that difficult that you need such heavy books?'

'Not necessarily, ma'am. The ninth through eleventh gen elevators used these gyrocoils that apparently could cycle energy infinitely by affecting how light and electromagnetic waves behaved inside of a special non-Gaussian electric field.'

Johnson could almost hear Mrs Belsinth's brain grind to a halt as they walked into the elevator and headed for the family room. He chuckled and continued. 'Very fascinating science, but it never really worked properly, so it was abandoned. The scientist that developed them could never figure out how to cause the gyrocoils to project their effects outward rather than inward, and though they briefly tried building the things at a scale where the space inside them was sufficient, ergo, the ninth through eleventh gen elevator, it was just impractical. The twelfth to most recent fourteenth gens use the older, cheaper, and more stable gravitomag engines that everything else uses.'

Mrs Belsinth stared at him blankly. 'These, um, gyrocoils are bad?'

'They're not bad. Well, the electric field seemed to interfere with clocks and timers, but nothing too serious. Worst case scenario, your watch is slower by a few minutes. It just didn't lead anywhere. Gyrocoils are a dead science. They were only researched for about a year. Everything with gyrocoils in them has been scrapped and replaced. I was shocked to see that your house had one, which is why I went looking for the book. I'm probably one of the only people besides the author that still own a copy.'

'Oh, dear,' Mrs Belsinth said, looking around the elevator like it had grown teeth. 'Hyacinth has a lot of explaining to do. I didn't know we kept dead science around the kids. We just liked the floatiness, so we turned down the agency when they came to replace the elevators five years ago. If I had known, I'd have forced Hyacinth to get rid of them.'

Johnson sensed an opportunity. 'Oh, you should be proud of them, Mrs Belsinth.' He reached out and stroked the elevator wall. The ridged surface spoke of where grooves had been cut into the metal to fit the gyrocoils. 'They may be a bit harder to repair, and only real specialists like myself can claim to truly understand them, but yours is perhaps the only mansion in Owerri that has one. Perhaps the only mansion in Nigeria. Africa? The world? Who knows? These elevators are truly unique, maybe even antique.'

'Antique?' Mrs Belsinth's eyes widened. 'Hyacinth and I, we've always been collectors. We have this authentic set of cutleries made from the bones of the last blue whale to ever exist. They're extinct now, you know, the poor things. If this elevator is special, well, are you sure it won't cause any harm to the kids, Mr Elevator Johnson?'

The elevator dinged and opened, revealing the messy family room and the oak table in a corner.

'Gyrocoils are a hundred per cent safe, ma'am, I assure you. They were abandoned for practicality, not safety. But what truly great piece of art is practical?'

'That is wonderful, Mr Elevator Johnson if you say so. I can't wait to tell Hyacinth. He would love to show it off. I am glad we have a specialist who can help us maintain the thing. Anyway, here's your book.'

'It would be a pleasure to continue to offer my services, ma'am,' Johnson said as they approached the table.

The heavy tome lay surrounded by other books. It was ostensibly a textbook to help engineers understand and repair gyrocoil elevators. But in reality, the book went into excruciating detail about the development of gyrocoils—the author's last-ditch effort to preserve some record of her research into a technology that was all but discarded.

Johnson reached out to grab the book and—

Elevator Johnson, in boxer shorts, leaned over the low rail on the balcony of his apartment on the 232nd floor and flashed his barcoded forearm at the idling drone watching from just inside the troposphere over Century Plaza, Owerri. He could not see it, only those on the 400th floor had ever claimed to glimpse the thing, but the green luminescence that flashed over his barcode signalled that it saw him, and that was all that mattered. It would send him his taxi.

He walked back into the apartment and started to throw his clothes back on. His digiset display was full of the news. All sixty-nine, no, seventeen streams he could afford, greeted him with the same boring image of an ethnically generic man and woman in grey or black or blue suits discussing the same breaking news—aliens. Which was a shame because he had wanted to see Caillou.

He took the gravitomag elevator down to the ground floor. Oddly, he felt disappointed in the ride. It seemed to lack floatiness. Johnson found his taxi waiting for him the moment he left the building.

'Elevator Johnson Mbadiwe?' The hip twenty-something driver called out.

'Yes. That's me.'

'Cool. Mind if I get confirmation from above?'

Johnson's head snapped up to the sky. In the corner of his eye, he seemed to see something descend to the earth, flying, but not like planes using superdense iron to manipulate gravity and magnetism. This thing flew by cycling energy and electricity, by changing the way it behaved inside a . . . something. The image was gone before he could make sense of it, and the driver was calling out to him. He shook his head and flashed his forearm at the drone in the sky.

'Sweet.' The driver grinned. 'God approves.'

Johnson shook his head and got in the backseat.

'What?' The driver asked with an even bigger smile. 'You don't believe in the big guy?'

Johnson provided an apologetic smile.

'Oh, I understand. It's okay, man. The big guy reaches us all differently. Besides,' the driver laughed, 'God may not exist. But aliens sure do.'

On the billboards suspended above the streets of Owerri, one clip played over and over again. Alien ships, floating through the inner Van Allen belt in a tight cycling orbit, unravelling dozens of artificial gravitomagnetic defences by changing the way they behaved.

Fifteen minutes later, Johnson walked out of the taxi and into the Horizon Beta Home Complex. Real gravel crunched under his thick rubber boots as he made his way to Beta 109 and rang the bell. The display on the door had sixty-nine streams. Johnson decided he really wanted sixty-nine streams. He'd go hungry to afford them if he had to.

All sixty-nine streams blinked out and were replaced by a face. Elevator Johnson's mind went blank. He did not recognize this face.

'Good afternoon, Mrs Belsinth.' The words left his mouth before he realized they were wrong.

The face beamed at him. 'You're the elevator guy.'

'You're not Mrs Belsinth.'

'No. I'm the new housekeeper. Mrs Belsinth is at an antique show with Mr Belsinth. You've fixed the elevators this morning, Mr Johnson. And they work. There's nothing wrong with them,' she said.

'Y-yes, ma'am. Your elevators are fine.'

'So, why are you here, Elevator Man?'

'Elevator Johnson, ma'am. I'm sorry to bother you, but I'm here because I left something behind. A textbook I had with me when I came this morning.' He struggled to recall the name. 'On the repair, no, on the mechanics of ninth through eleventh generation gyroelectrically stable elevators by Trisha Kingsley. I think I left it on the oak table in the family room.'

There was a tense silence, and then, 'Give me a moment.'

The ping of the elevators came through the speakers, and the display switched back to showing sixty-nine streams.

Johnson felt . . . off. He'd felt off throughout today, done things that made no sense. He regretted bringing the book with him. He hadn't needed it. It was a wiring issue.

Conversation filtered from the streams into Johnson's ears. A bleak-looking news anchor on one stream interrogated a dark-haired bespectacled scientist.

'Dr Okorafor, ma'am, the experts on the internet forums are calling your theory bullshit. Isn't this just a polite way of saying we can't stop them?'

'Frank, that kind of thinking is why world governments have yet to send out forces to meet them. We're relying on passive defences that clearly don't work against this technology instead of hitting them with ours and seeing how they fare.'

'I never thought I'd see the space scientists be the ones clamouring for offensive measures.'

'The aliens have not been polite, Frank. Maybe if we hit them with something, someone on board will say hello.'

The voices from the TV cut off sharply as every one of the sixty-nine streams switched to the same live news update. The aliens had just exited low orbit at high speed and entered the upper ionosphere. And they had sent a radio signal. They were initiating first contact.

The news blinked away, and the housekeeper's apologetic face reappeared on the door's display.

'Mr Johnson, there were so many books on that table. Mrs Belsinth was tired of complaining and asked me to clear them away. I kept the ones that belonged to the kids and to Mr Belsinth, but I'm not sure about yours.'

'Ma'am, my book is specifically, *On the Mechanics of Ninth Through Eleventh Generation—*,'

'Oh, I know. I think I saw it, which is why I'm apologizing. Maybe you should come see for yourself.'

'Yes, ma'am.' Johnson sighed with relief. He pressed his arm against the display.

'What are you doing?'

'I'm verifying my identity.'

'Oh, there's no need for that. I recognise you.'

The door slid open, and Johnson walked into the mansion to find the housekeeper walking out of an elevator to meet him.

'I'm truly sorry. If only I had known the book was yours.' She wrung her hands and herded Johnson into the elevator.

The elevator started up. Johnson placed a hand on its walls, and the smooth, grooveless metal unsettled him. 'It's a gravitomagnetic elevator,' Johnson said, frowning.

'Yes. Why wouldn't it be?' The housekeeper stared at him.

'I don't know. I just thought it would be . . . unique.'

The elevator dinged and opened, revealing the tidy family room and the oak table in a corner.

In another corner, an electric fireplace, now turned off, smouldered and wafted smoke.

The heavy tome lay burned, surrounded by other books and loose garbage.

'I'm sorry, Mr Johnson, but by the time I turned it off, it had already been ruined. I'm sure Mrs Belsinth will fully compensate you.'

Johnson nodded and sighed. Then he shook his head, his gaze sharpening.

'There's something not right. The book, I'm trying to recall its content. It's about . . . gyrocoils. I know how they work.'

The housekeeper sucked in a breath. 'Mr Johnson, listen.'

The digiset in another corner of the room came alive with sixty-nine streams. The content on all of them was the same.

'The radio broadcast received from the alien ships a few minutes ago, just before they landed in Washington DC and New York, has been leaked. We now broadcast the message in its entirety.'

'Hello, Earth. Be not afraid. For most of you, we come in peace. This is a colonial endeavour. We intend to lay a small mining claim to your corner of the universe. To achieve this, we will be invading the United States of America. We had to choose one country on your planet, and our tacticians who have crawled your webspace and searched your media informed the Invasion Council that invading the United States was, and we quote, "full of irony" and "they're going to love this." We hope that by invading in line with your popular culture, we have earned your goodwill. We thank The Hollywood for providing us surprisingly accurate information about your extraterrestrial defences.'

The broadcast buzzed once like it had ended before starting again.

'Finally, to the good engineer who has given us such a headache, we say, "Don't. You have fixed the elevator. Go home."'

The broadcast cut off, and the display went silent.

Elevator Johnson took the elevator out of Beta 109. The gravel underfoot felt like hot coals, searing him through his rubber boots. He flashed his forearm at the sky and hailed a taxi to Century Plaza, Owerri. The elevator ride up was not floaty. He secured the lock on his front door and the latch on his balcony entrance. Elevator Johnson Mbadiwe took off his clothes and curled up in his bed, then called up his seventeen streams and watched Caillou on all of them until he fell asleep.

THAT OVER WHICH THEY'D DISPUTE
Lubwama Johnson

She found him cowering at the edge of the pine forest one afternoon on her way home from school, half occupying a hole in the earth he couldn't possibly have dug himself, choosing to turn his face away when she crossed over to that side of the road.

'Athieno is my name,' she whispered, bending over the puppy.

'You're doing what?' her brother asked, looking back at her.

'Home can we take him?'

'Dog is wild, Athieno.'

'No, he isn't. I want to keep him.'

She wondered how many people had bypassed him. She passed her index finger along the edge of his right ear and felt him tremble. He was much too young to already be suspicious of the world.

She couldn't stop thinking about him. It was already getting dark. She went out to the kitchen and picked out the lightest sack, tucked it under her blouse and slowly slipped away.

'Puncture it.'

'What?'

'It won't breathe. Puncture the sack.'

When she just stood there, her brother walked over to her and held out his hand, looking from her face to her abdomen. She took out the sack and handed it over. A good four times, he folded it neatly, ever so carefully, well aware of the rules of symmetry. He then anchored it onto his raised thigh and drew a small knife from around his waist, cutting out numerous almost perfectly circular holes through it. When he spread it out forcefully so it slapped the wind, she saw that the holes in the sack were lined out in regular intervals like a factory setting, like they had shipped with the sack. She smiled at him and said thank you.

'A dog house please help me raise,' she asked Sunny the next day.

'Dog it's not even yours.'

'Nobody wants him. Grow up he will, and then protect us.'

'Protect us from what?' he countered, grinning and leaning forward, reaching for the knife around his waist and brandishing it so that it sliced through the air back and forth, inches from her face. When he saw she wasn't impressed, he put it back into its sheath.

'For a month I will wash the utensils.'

He squinted at her, half confused, half surprised. He leaned back and belched loudly.

'A month, you say? Starting when?'

'Where's the soap?'

Athieno got up from the floor.

Their house was diminutive. She always daydreamed of making a fortune and buying her mother a lakeside mansion. But the older she had gotten, the more she'd come to suspect that a stupid fancy house—with ten, even twenty, daily chocolate bars for every bruise on her mother's face—couldn't make up for all those years. And that was her face alone. Her mother's body was a gallery of splendid scars that nobody but the artist was permitted to behold.

Athieno snuck out of her bedroom that night, a one-window

earth-floored room with no ceiling, just like the other rooms, which she shared with her elder brother, Sunny. All of the other rooms, apart from the marital bedroom of course, which she imagined was much improved, with its supposed sanctity, a room into which she had never stared. A cold wind was howling in their ungazetted compound, and it would've been dark all around had the moon not decided to come out in its entirety. When she approached him at the left flank of the house where she had left him, he sensed her, and the sack came alive, which brought her much joy. Movement was just the vital sign she was looking for. When she held him in both hands, he smelled of the wild and, for his minuteness, seemed a little braver than their previous encounter. They were already making acquaintance. She left him there, eyes glowing, and when she returned from the kitchen, she had a bowl of meat.

That over which they'd dispute, she knew not. All she and Sunny would hear were raised voices—sometimes screams—through those paper-thin walls. It was a weekend tradition for their parents to disagree on matters of seemingly national importance. If correctly stated, they consistently failed terribly at diplomacy. But there were better days too sometimes, those dwindling mercurial highs, such moments to behold, like their glad conversations on the front porch on Sunday mornings, as though nothing had transpired the night before. Quite frankly, Athieno didn't know resilience to mean anything besides that woman. Yes, half of the world's resilience quite possibly slept at their house, in the shared body of a kind-hearted soul, her mother.

'Heard the maize, they won't buy.'

'We can wait out the season.'

'Every season we need money.' Father's hand swung forward, projecting the splint he had been picking his teeth with.

'Next week we can sell. Higher prevailing price everywhere.'

'And this week?'

When Mother didn't answer, opting to stare into the distance, Father pulled out his wallet, a beaten leather wallet, once brown, now discoloured.

'Twenty thousand shillings,' he announced like she couldn't differentiate between banknotes.

She tugged at her hair and smiled, and it wasn't synthetic, plastic. Then the dog whimpered.

'That's what?' Father inquired. Mother didn't reply, and her blank stare was evidence enough that she knew no better than he did.

Father got up and followed the whimpering, and Athieno, who had been busying herself in the kitchen, appeared in the doorway.

'Dog, whose is it?'

Nobody answered him.

'Said me, dog, whoever it is for?' He was shouting.

'Dog, he is mine.'

He looked in Athieno's direction, his eyes imploring her to continue.

'They gave me him week before this one. They friends near Capital.'

'They friends near Capital?'

'Yes.'

'So, they friends near Capital you love more, or your father next bedroom?' He was holding his waist.

'My father next bedroom.'

'Then hear me, girl. There be no liking for dogs within me.'

He looked at the dog again, closer. 'And I ain't never seen no such dog, all where I go.'

So then, the matter was settled. She was to return the dog, no questions asked.

Although not entirely unexpected, Father's directive changed everything. The two children had to find a new location for the dog house, far removed from their house. The pine forest two hundred yards behind their house covered much of what anybody could see for a mile or so, and it's what Athieno thought of first. It wasn't the safest spot, let alone the most convenient, but Father would undoubtedly kill the dog if he encountered him again. It took two weeks, but the dog house was completed. It stood a metre high, made of naked wooden poles and rusty iron sheets, and sandwiched between two pine trees that miraculously broke the wind whilst also providing shelter. Athieno thanked God for her brother's genius. She borrowed money for a padlock from a friend at school, who jokingly asked what valuable thing she owned and wanted to lock away if she couldn't even afford a padlock.

'To the town help me take him. All dogs they are injected these days.' She was pleading with Sunny. Sunny was mute. He kept drawing lines in the dust.

'Look, money when I get, I will give. You help me.'

No response.

'And worry none. I have bathed him.'

'Please, man—'

Sunny stood up, taking his time about it. He was two heads taller than her. He moved towards her, took the keys from her hand, and scanned the horizon.

'Why all this you're doing?'

'All what?'

'All this. Dog, it isn't yours. Us, we're poor, Athieno. Dog, it's high breed, obvious that one. It will grow, and because little meat you have, it will hate you.'

'Sounding like Father, you are.' When Sunny digested that, he bowed his head, handed back the keys and turned to enter the house. She had to go to the town by herself.

On the way to the town, she daydreamed of the owners intercepting her, and then wondered why they would come for the dog now, after not once bothering for three months. The vet's chubby cheeks excited the girl. She wanted to touch them so badly. When it was finally her turn so that he moved over to examine the dog, he squinted at the creature and backed away. He then asked her as courteously as he could, 'Where did you get this?'

'You mean what?'

'Is this your dog, girl?'

She overheard him on the phone in the laboratory talking to somebody. What was it? Animal Control. Yes, wolf eyes. Yes, come check it. Yes, 114, Gundaba Lane. Yes, Dr Wangani. She tiptoed to where the vet had placed the dog and grabbed it. It made no sound, thankfully. She scanned the floor for the sack she had brought him in, but it wasn't anywhere to be seen. She tucked him under her arm, supporting his weight with both her hands. Then she ran. She slipped under somebody's outstretched arm in the doorway and didn't watch the traffic. She ran as fast as her lungs could fuel her legs until she got to a turn off the main road. She was panting, but the dog was calm. She spotted a trench. When she found the courage to look back and saw no pursuant, Athieno crawled into the trench, dumping the dog in first.

The girl was catching her breath, studying the dog's facial features. Its teeth were so sharp, but so were every dog's. And the gums, they were a ghastly pale purple. Purple gums. Purple, not pink, not red. She promised to read about that at school the next day. Sitting in the trench, Athieno thought back to everything. The dog was looking up at her face as though imploring her to share her troubles with it, if she didn't mind.

'Home now we cannot go. Missed school to inject you.' The dog kept looking on, unsatisfied.

'But a story I can tell you in the meantime,' she conceded.

*

Father often told people that the little Catholic faith he had in his tired heart was reserved for Easter celebrations. It was his favourite time of the year, the only other time he got to stay away from the docks on weekdays and be home with his family. The other such time was Christmas, but that was universal. You didn't need to be Catholic or Christian to make merry in December. For Easter Sundays, he'd invite a bunch of old men over, mostly old friends and widowers and people that he knew to share in his obsession for good traditional food. He'd sit them in the compound, and they'd talk politics, and it was no less sophisticated a topic even when it concerned a village that small, a village that didn't appear on most maps. Then the aroma from the kitchen would diffuse its way to their ancient nostrils, and Father would be right in the centre of the space, loving the attention, reminding them all of how good a cook his wife was. But they surely knew that. They surely knew that. If anybody asked Athieno, she'd say the previous Easter had been a really beautiful one, mostly because discussing many past events in their family no doubt called for selective recollection, if not for the pleasure of her father, then for the preservation of her own sanity, a thing already so delicate.

The aroma had originated from the kitchen, and Mother had conjured it. She had brought forth the food, and Athieno had helped her carry it. The men eyed the young girl like she was part of the course. Disgusting old men with no religion. Mother was asked to stay, and Athieno was sent on her way. But she didn't stray so far, watching from behind the house. One of the men remarked that Father was getting old, and so Father wanted to prove himself. He thought for a bit and then saw that Mother could help him, thank you very much.

'I have a question that's yours, Mama.'

'Mister, yes?'

'Am I getting old, Mama?'

'You aren't, no.'

'Getting old in some way, don't lie?'

'You aren't, no.' She was focused on serving the food.

'Then good, done.' Father looked at his friends, one after the other.

Then he suddenly caught Mother's right hand in a tight grip, forcing her to look up at him.

'No, Mama. Convinced they not, I see. We again try. You tell them now.'

'Tell them what, mister?' She had stopped serving the food. The men were watching, eyeing one another, waiting.

'Our nights together, you tell them about.'

'Pardon, mister?'

'You don't ask. Our nights together, you tell them.'

Mother didn't respond. From her face, Athieno could tell she was embarrassed.

'Okay, okay. Getting old in some way, you lied.' Father shook her wrist back and forth.

'No, I lie not, mister. Nights together, I love so much. Youthful as ever you are, mister.' There was an urgency to her tone, Mother.

'Okay. Anything else need telling, you go on now.'

'Mister, I—'

'You what, Mama?'

'Mister, I—' She didn't have the words.

'Okay. Food losing hotness now. You will tell them next Easter, won't you?' He had that twisted face.

'I will, mister, I will.'

Father looked at Mother in disbelief and forcefully let go of her wrist.

When Mother came out of the circus, Athieno thought she had dodged a bullet. She helped her clean the house. That night, when the old men were all gone, scattered, and it was just Father and Mother, and Athieno and Sunny who were irrelevant, he beat her so bad. He beat her up for embarrassing him, that she had hesitated to back him. That she didn't ever listen.

Athieno was sweating and hungry, and she imagined her dog was feeling the same way. She had to find her way home somehow and explain her return from school earlier than usual.

On the last Saturday of February, as Father sundried in the compound, Athieno had to find a way to get to the dog, like she always did every weekend when the man was home. The only difference this time was that he hadn't budged since midmorning, basking in the hot sun like it wouldn't shine the next day. Looking at him, she withdrew into her mind. He was never intoxicated. But how she wished it were different. It would've helped with the utter helplessness she always felt when she couldn't run to Mother's rescue when things weren't going well in that bedroom. How she wished he drank. At least she would have something tangible to point fingers at. Something.

'To where, girl?'

'They friends near Capital.'

'Oh?'

'Yeah.'

'Come around little, please.'

Fidgeting her dress, she moved to where he was. Without so much as a word, he grabbed her, felt around her waist for a good ten seconds, and some knots came undone. He wasn't even awkward about it. He didn't need to be. He was only grazing his daughter. He looked at the ground without blinking. Dried pieces of meat had fallen from around Athieno's waist, wrapped in banana fibre. Two identical keys on a plastic holder, too.

'Fancy keys, I see. It open to where, girl?'

She hesitated.

'It open to where, please say?'

'They friends near Capital.'

'Oh? I see. Starving lot are they too?' He was still looking down at the pieces of meat on the ground.

'We just eat together.'

'I mind not, don't worry. Would never call it a bad thing, charity. Only concern here is fancy keys.'

She didn't know what to say.

'Have not been to Capital since forever, actually.' Father picked up the keys. 'We go together, both of us. What do you say?'

'They are young, they friends,' Athieno bargained.

'So, I'm old, eh?'

'No, but they young people under you.'

'Okay. Won't bother none your young friends, eh? Just want to see fancy padlock, done.'

Father watched her, and when Athieno felt the stab of his stare, she nodded. Her heart was racing. Father got up, screamed at Mother he'd be back soon, and off they went.

'Long route the one you're using, I see.'

Capital wasn't in the direction of the pine forest, and everybody knew that. He was trailing her, toe for toe. When they got to the edge of the pine forest, she didn't pretend to go by the route along it because she knew that would be the end of her. Even from ten steps ahead, she could hear her father's heavy breathing. She held her breath and cornered into the forest. Father trailed her in silence. Perhaps none of it surprised him. The leaves rustled twice as loud under the weight of his heavy-duty boots, the ones he never took off, even at home. They approached the dog house, and the dog let out a low, sustained growl. Then, suddenly, Athieno realised something. She had never heard the dog bark before. Never, ever. Only growls and howls, maybe whimpering. But there were other, no doubt, more urgent things to worry about now. She touched the dog house and looked back. Father had a stupid grin, but his eyes were serious.

'They friends near Capital,' he whispered menacingly. He flung the keys to her. Athieno opened the dog house and let him out.

'Lord Jesus, what is that, girl?'

She looked back at Father, and the sheer horror on his face surprised her. When she released the dog from her grip, it made for Father, who instantly backed to a tree. Athieno grabbed the dog around its abdomen and held it back.

'What is that? What is that? What, what, what—'

The dog growled again, and Athieno understood that Father was an unwelcome visitor.

'You stay here, understand?' he commanded her when he had finally managed to straighten his face. It was the most uneasy she had ever seen him.

Father walked home as fast as his legs could carry him. Athieno knew he was going to fetch the appropriate means to kill her dog. She stroked his jawbone. The silvery-white fur almost glowed in the artificial shade of the pine forest. She was going to miss him. She scanned the place and then looked down at her dog. She could always let him go, send him away. At least he'd still be breathing. She didn't want to, but she had to. She let go of the dog, walked over to a branch lying on the forest floor, and approached him. He didn't yield an inch. She waved the branch before his face, and he thought it was their newfound game. He wasn't much for games, but he could try this once. Athieno paused, closed her eyes and kept inching closer. She got to where the dog was, quickly hoisted the branch, and struck him across the face between his eyes. He jumped backwards in pain, whimpering. His chest swelled like he was preparing to charge at her, but she knew he couldn't. A trickle of red ran down his head, sharply contrasting with the white of his fur. She didn't have time. She charged forward again and aimed to strike him in the same place, but the dog's instincts were heightened. He ducked sideways, and she missed, falling to the ground on her palms. She got up and turned to face the dog again. She felt around for the branch in the fallen leaves. When she found it and brandished it, he started howling, the loudest she'd ever heard him howl. She approached him a third time, and this time, he turned and ran so swiftly. She watched him disappear among the trees and felt her knees give way.

In the evening, Sunny found Athieno seated on the edge of the pine forest, palms tucked under her chin, crying. He approached her and sat himself down beside her.

'Sister, I'm sorry.'

He had brought her food. When she pushed it away, he said, 'A dog I don't think it was, Athieno. Go home let us.'

It. Sunny didn't think it was a dog. She didn't know if the cold food or the wrong pronoun broke her heart more.

In the evening, still, she sat by herself in the kitchen. Mother stood in the doorway and observed her for ages, then walked back into the compound, returning with a wooden stool. 'Your dog, I'm sorry.' She reached for her hand.

'All right, it is. Never was mine, dog.'

'Warned you, I should have.'

Athieno looked at her, surprised, and then they were both staring at each other.

'You mean what?' Mother didn't respond. Athieno looked away.

'How did you know, Mama?' she said, almost whispering.

'Well . . . well, two children I have, don't I? There's a type of worry that only children they can bring, and in the case of yours, a dog. Your face always it was like that.' She squeezed Athieno's hand. Nobody spoke for a discomforting while.

'Why don't you get another child?'

'Wish I could, I do.' She thought to ask Mother to elaborate and then decided against it.

Two months went by, and she still wondered where he was. It was Easter, and with it came the usual gathering, the usual imbeciles.

'Mama, you haven't shed one beauty, yes!' one stupid man remarked.

'Carefully, Bimba. Bones of your mother I'll dig up and sleep with.' It was Father.

The silly smirk evaporated from Bimba's face.

'Mama, do you know to women God listens more?' Father asked.

'No, mister.'

'Well, He do. Why though, wouldn't tell. Maybe you know why, Mama?'

'I know not, mister.'

'But you know to cook, don't you?'

'Yes, mister. To cook I try.'

'Okay Mama, you pray for this our food, yes.'

She prayed for the food. Her voice was unsteady like she was fighting the temptation to call down poison from Heaven.

'You go now, Mama. Appreciate all of us do.'

Mother got up to leave, and then somebody spoke up.

'Will she return to tell us story?'

'What story, comfortable man?' Father grimaced at the man.

'Oh, yes. Last year Easter. You remember not?' It was Bimba. The loose-lipped man had jumped at the chance.

'Oh, yes. Last year Easter. I eager for that one,' somebody else echoed.

'Did you forgive her, mister? You softer than I remember, dock-man.' They all laughed.

Mother was still there standing, her back to them. She was told to take a seat.

On the front porch in the evening, Athieno looked up to the stars. She was thinking of her dog. She missed him so. She hadn't even given him a name. She was thinking the stars were no match for his eyes, the way they illuminated in the dark. Then she heard raised voices. There was only one place they could've been coming from. In the living room, she joined Sunny, who was seated by his pocket radio, listening. Athieno didn't understand why he was so oblivious to the violence. Was it because he was a boy, very soon a man? The voices in the marital bedroom were increasing by the minute. Why was he unperturbed? She had confronted him once, and he had said that he had been present at a time when their parents never so much as argued, but things had changed when a girl was born into the family. And she was the only girl.

You bloody bitch! You don't listen. Ungrateful. Ungrateful. Had it coming. Going to kill you. Two children you only give me.

They heard the sound of breaking glass and Mother screaming.

I'm not old, I'll show you.

Of course it had been a year, and of course Mother hadn't found the words yet. Poor Mama. She was screaming. Then silence. Then she was screaming again. Something bumped into a wall and shook the house at its foundations. 'Not today,' Athieno thought to herself. She tiptoed into the corridor. A shadow was darting back and forth from the crevice below their parents' door. She turned swiftly and dashed across the corridor into the living room. She reached for the lantern, much to Sunny's puzzlement, and ran out of the house.

She sprinted into the night, not looking back. Sunny pursued her but stopped at the edge of their compound, from where he just looked on. Athieno was seeing everything blurry on a fogless night. It was the fish-eyed lenses of her tear-stained eyes. And then beads were rolling down those eyes; fat, succulent beads. The flame of the lantern was flickering in the cold of the night. She reached the edge of the pine forest. The whistle of the trees and the smell of coniferous wood greeted her, but she didn't greet them back. Her mind was all over the place. It was Easter. They were supposed to be celebrating. Jesus was rising. Why then was Mama falling? But maybe that's how things were. Maybe to truly be a man, you had to constantly remind: I built the house, didn't I? I buy the food, don't I? I'm stronger than you, aren't I? You're just a bloody woman, aren't you? Rhetorical questions the man spat out with the sort of urgency the woman couldn't match, and then he was beating her all over again. Yes, maybe to be a man, you had to demolish and rebuild lest you lose your touch; you had to break, but never so bad that you wouldn't be able to mend. To truly be a man, Athieno, you had to constantly remind, lest they forget.

But she had never given him a name. What would she use to summon him? Then she thought. She thought like a mother. The girl screamed at the top of her lungs.

'Athieno!'

'Athieno!'

Nothing.

Using a splint, she borrowed light from the lantern and set a few rusty leaves on fire. She kept calling out. She was desperate. The leaves burned out because they weren't dry enough. She moved further east, or whatever direction. There, the leaves were drier, but so was her throat. She called out again.

'Athieno!'

'Athieno!'

She listened closely. For movement. Howling. Anything. Nothing, nothing but the trees swaying and distant frogs croaking. She hung her face low in disappointment. What had she expected? Athieno was her name.

She slouched home, lantern swinging like a pendulum. She walked, wiping the tears with the back of her hand. Then she heard a distant growl behind her. She looked back. Nothing. Where was it coming from? She traced the growl, blindly.

'Athieno!'

She heard a rushed rustle of leaves. Something was heeding the call. She held the lantern to her face and watched. The charging stopped behind a tree, metres ahead of her. She hadn't seen much, but she had seen the white. She approached the tree.

'Athieno,' she loudly whispered. It took him forever, but he stepped into the light of the lantern. There he was, eyes shinier than ever. He was so big and tall, maybe the height of her waist. Had he reconsidered their friendship? He looked disappointed that she came bearing no gifts, no meat, but he also looked sorry, apologetic. They both had something to be sorry about. She wondered if there were more of him out there. She straightened the lantern when the smell of paraffin hit her nostrils. The lantern had been spilling.

The dog regarded her with contempt like she had overstepped the terms of their divorce, a divorce that hadn't truly been consensual. But she had no time. They could always catch up. She turned and broke into a run. She knew he'd follow. Almost at the edge of the forest, she tripped and fell, the lantern falling and rolling yards away from her. She didn't retrieve it. She kept running, her son beside her.

The moon was their company. Reminded her of their first day. The day she stuffed him in a sack. It was a moonlit night as well. The girl kept running. She was at her compound. She burst through the front door, straight to the bedroom. Not her bedroom. It was the bedroom with the paper-thin walls, the one with a sanctity to it.

Father was still upon Mother, and the two were shocked to see Athieno. There was a look of horror on Father's face that Athieno didn't have the time to analyse because the animal was already upon the man, going for his neck. The dog hugged Father until they were both falling, Father at the bottom of the heap. The dog pinned him down. Everybody was screaming. Father tried to wrestle him off, but he was a big dog, a dog the waist height of the girl. Athieno watched in horror, and so did Mother, who was too transfixed to move a limb. The dog's teeth tugged at Father's neck repeatedly. They were bumping into things. Then Father's hand was slipping off the dog's back, slowly. Dramatically. He was grunting and taking low breaths, tearing away at Father's neck. The earth was doing its best to soak up the glistening red, but most of Father's blood was already meeting Mother's. And now there was blood everywhere. Out in the distance, a cloud of smoke was spreading over.

THE AUTHORS

Charlie Muhumuza is a Ugandan writer and lawyer. His works have appeared in Lolwe, adda, Isele and other literary magazines. His short stories have been recognized in writing competitions such as the Afritondo short story prize (2021, 2023), The Commonwealth short story prize (2021, 2022) and the Kalahari short story prize (2020). He is a believer in imagination and is curious about our worlds.

C. M. Okonkwo is a French-speaking award-winning Nigerian author who grew up in Lagos and moved to France to study, where she obtained three degrees in Business Management, Personnel and Employment Management, and International HR Management and Development. An associate member of the Chartered Institute of Personnel Management of Nigeria, she currently practices HR as a profession and writes as a passion. She has self-published more than 30 books across various categories (prose, poetry, play) and genres (crime, thriller, literary fiction, erotica, romance, horror, science fiction, fantasy, and nonfiction), some of which have been shortlisted for awards and also won prizes, including the Africa Book Club Short Story Competition (winner), the 50 Best Indie Books (two-time finalist), Quramo Writers' Prize (two-time finalist), Wattpad Short Story Contest (multiple-time winner), the African Writers Award (poetry longlist), Itanile Award (winner), and the Canopus Awards for Interstellar Writing (finalist). Her works have also appeared in LitArt Magazine, SprinNG Eros Anthology, PEN Nigeria Anthology, and Itanile Magazine.

Alex Kadiri writes from Lagos, Nigeria. He is a graduate of English and Literary Studies and has been longlisted or shortlisted for Stories of the Nature of Cities, Koffi Addo Prize for Nonfiction, Awele Creative Trust, Problem House Press, Toyin Falola Prize, Afritondo Short Story Prize etc. He has contributed fiction at ShortSharpShort, WordsAreWork, Whipik, Afreada, Writivism (And Morning Will Come Anthology), Afritondo (Rain Dance Anthology) and has others forthcoming in the ANA Nest of Tales Anthology, Lunaris Review and elsewhere. Alex won the Quramo Writers' Prize 2020 and is the author of Sunshower, a product of his award-winning manuscript. While he humours the voices in his head that prognosticate a literary future where he becomes a force to be reckoned with, Alex currently attempts to tell familiar stories in unfamiliar ways. His hobbies include binge-watching movies, reading quality fiction and (of course) writing. Occasionally, he challenges chess players from around the world, or just goes swimming.

Ayo Awoyungbo scribbles a few lines every day, even if they can't be shared with anyone else. Sometimes, he edits and saves them. Other times he simply deletes. On that basis, he describes himself as a writer. He was tempted to make up a list of imaginary literary prizes he has won, been longlisted for, or been shortlisted for, as well as non-existent publications that have recognised his short fiction, but after mulling it over, he decided against it, as these things can be checked. You will not find him on Facebook or Twitter. Or Instagram. Or LinkedIn. But this doesn't mean he has no friends.

Desta Haile is a multilingual British-Eritrean writer and educator with a background in intercultural communication, social justice and the performing arts. In 2020 Desta won To Speak Europe in Different Languages at Babel Festival of Literature and Translation, a writing competition organised by Asmara-Addis Literary Festival (In Exile), Specimen Press, and the European Cultural Foundation for her story York to Tehran. In 2021, she received the Afritondo short story prize for her story Ethio-Cubano. Her passion project, Languages through Music, was awarded a BOZAR Afropolitan Forum grant for its innovation, and has developed workshops and resources for festivals like Africa Utopia at Southbank Centre. As a musician, she composed the UNESCO Green Citizens campaign song and has worked with artists like Joe Bataan, Zap Mama, and Baloji. She holds an MA in Black British Writing from Goldsmiths, University of London. Desta is currently the Deputy Director of the Royal African Society.

Ani Kayode Somtochukwu is an award-winning Nigerian writer and queer liberation activist. His work interrogates themes of queer identity, resistance and liberation, and has been shortlisted for the 2020 ALCS TOM-Gallon Trust Award and the 2022 Toyin Falola Prize. He won the 2021 James Currey Prize for African Literature for his debut novel, And Then He Sang a Lullaby, which will be published by Roxane Gay Books in June 2023.

Lubwama Joshua is a writer from Kampala, Uganda. He is the editor-in-chief of Inverbally, an African digital literary magazine, and a co-founder at Rhivaly Media, a media and entertainment start-up.

Uchechi Princewill is a fiction writer and medical student at the University of Benin, Nigeria. His writing explores the motions of living beings, real and fantastical. His work has appeared or is forthcoming in The Bombay Literary Magazine, Litro Magazine, The Story Tree Challenge Maiden Anthology, and Pikes Peak Writers Dream Anthology. He is also a regional winner of the 2017 Commonwealth Youth Council Poetry Competition. He can be found in most spaces @bryanwhoiam.

Jenny Robson was born in South Africa, but has lived in her beloved Botswana since the age of 22. She works as a music teacher in Maun, writing in her spare time. Most of her stories have been for children and young adults. One of them was awarded the international UNESCO Prize for Youth Literature in the Service of Tolerance. These days, Jenny is focused on writing for adults. She finds this far more challenging and intimidating. In 2021 one of her adult stories was awarded the Kendeka Prize for African Literature. This has motivated her to keep on trying.

Tafadzwa Taruvinga is a versatile fiction and nonfiction writer, and author of The Educated Waiter: Memoir of an African Immigrant—a powerful recollection of his quest to find a better life in South Africa, Germany, the UAE and Zimbabwe. Witty and poignant, this story confronts poverty, racism, xenophobia and classism. In 2021, Tafadzwa was awarded a scholarship by the Faculty of Humanities at the University of the Witwatersrand to study for an MA in Creative Writing and is completing his first novel set in urban and rural Zimbabwe. He is also the founder of a writing agency based in Johannesburg, South Africa. His research interest is in development economics with a focus on issues affecting and stemming from the movement of African migrants.

Igbẹkẹle Salawu's works have been published in literary magazines. In 2015, one of his published works was nominated for a Pushcart prize. In 2018, as an intern editor at the Oxford University Press, he participated in an extensive translation project aimed towards the development of a Yorùbá dictionary. He was a Fulbright scholar at the University of North Carolina at Chapel Hill between 2021 and 2022, after completing a graduate programme at the Institute of African Studies, University of Ibadan. He is now studying fiction at Florida State University.

Enit'ayanfe Ayosojumi Akinsanya is a Nigerian writer. He grew up in Sagamu. He is the recipient of the 2022 Itanile Africa/Diaspora Fiction Prize and the 2022 International Arts Lounge CNF First-Position Award. He was a finalist at the 2018 National GTB Dusty Manuscript Novel Contest and a fellow at the 2018 Farafina/Okadabooks Bootcamp. He is the author of a short story collection, "How to Catch a Story That Doesn't Exist", which weaves through the lives of queer Nigerians. The collection was published by IfeÁdigo in 2022. His other works have appeared in Kalahari Review, Brittle Paper, Isele Magazine, The Shallow Tales Review, Eunoia Review, Afrocritik, Fiery Scribe Review, Livina Press, Africa Writer, OBBLT, Writers Space Africa, CÓN-SCÌÒ and several other platforms. He is currently observing life and building lives in the southwest of Nigeria.

Fayssal Bensalah is a twenty-eight-year-old Algerian author who writes in English. He was born and raised in Algeria. He was educated at Constantine 1 University (C1U) and graduated with an MA degree in Anglophone Literature. He is currently finishing his PhD in critical and creative writing at Cardiff University, UK, where he also worked as a creative writing tutor. He is the winner of the inaugural 2020 Toyin Falola Prize. He co-judged the 2022 Toyin Falola Prize with Booker-Prize-nominated author Karen Jennings.

Moses Abukutsa writes poetry and fiction. He was shortlisted for the 2017 NALIF (Nyanza Literary Festival) literary prize for his short story Abraham's Cremation and recently longlisted for the 2022 Afritondo short story prize. Abukutsa Moses is also the winner of the 2022 Kikwetu Literary journal's flash fiction contest with his story Nalongo. He is also a member of WSA (Writers Space Africa)—Kenya chapter. He has published short stories and poetry online with Kalahari review, Praxis, African Writer, Kikwetu, Afritondo, Storymoja and khusoko.com an East African Online Business platform. Abukutsa is a high school teacher of English and Literature who likes reading and playing tennis during his free time. He lives in Western Kenya.

RECOMMENDED READING

The Hope, The Prayer, The Anthem
An Anthology

The Hope, The Prayer, The Anthem is a collection of short stories on identity, love, hope, and self-discovery. Told by rising and award-winning writers from across the African continent and beyond, the stories are a rich blend of suspense, humour, drama, and romance.

"... It is complex, exciting, full of surprises, and brimming with brilliance."
—Maneo Mohale, Author, Everything is s Deadly Flower

THE INSTITUTE FOR CREATIVE DYING
A Novel

On the slopes of Northcliff Ridge, below the second-highest vantage point in Johannesburg, ladybugs get ravaged by ants, ants are zombified by fungi, and fungi become the means for awakening. Above these stand an unnumbered house, protected by high walls and obscured by tall trees. Here five strangers meet, all of them yearning for a way through to the end of life as they have known it.

The Institute for Creative Dying is a colourful examination of human mortality amid botanical, technological, and animalic worlds. It is a story that explores the limits of living. One that asks whether it is possible to die before your death.

RECOMMENDED READING

Rain Dance
An Anthology

"The stories are surprising in the best ways, innovative, full of humour and unflinching. These are exciting voices I hope to continue hearing from." —'Pemi Aguda, Winner, Deborah Rogers Foundation Writers Award 2020.